ABOUT TH

Russell Mardell is a playwright, scriptwriter and filmmaker based in the South West of England. His debut collection of short fiction *Silent Bombs Falling on Green Grass* is also available.

For more information visit www.russellmardell.co.uk

STONE
BLEEDING

RUSSELL MARDELL

Matador
9 Priory Business Park
Wistow Road
Kibworth Beauchamp
Leicester LE8 0RX, UK
Tel: (+44) 116 279 2299
Fax: (+44) 116 279 2277
Email: books@troubador.co.uk
Web: www.troubador.co.uk/matador

ISBN 978 1780880 747

British Library Cataloguing in Publication Data.
A catalogue record for this book is available from the British Library.

Cover design by David Baker

"No Harm" © 2011
Written by Nathan Nicholson, Adam Harrison, Piers Hewitt and Todd Howe
Published by WMPI as agent for Primary Wave Brian (Boxer Rebellion Sp. Acct) (BMI)
All Rights Reserved, Used by Permission

Typeset in 11pt Gaillard BT by Troubador Publishing Ltd, Leicester, UK

Matador is an imprint of Troubador Publishing Ltd

Printed and bound in the UK by TJ International, Padstow, Cornwall

For my brothers Graham & Fergus
and my boxer brother Todd
Thank you

CONTENTS

Maybe there's no harm
There's no harm in you
So watch what you see
There's a beast that's in me

- The Boxer Rebellion, *No Harm*

Zach's Verse

In the beginning…

It was the business and the business was everything. Business was good and I was good and I was the best in the business. Even in this troubled country of ours, there is something glorious in being good, being professional and being the best. Even if it only really matters to none but yourself and at no point other than those horrible waking hours where you try and remember who you are and reflection comes at you like the bony hand of a pervert, it is still important and it still has relevance. I may be plying my trade in a lunatic's marketplace but I firmly believe that even lunatics appreciate talent and professionalism. It was easier at the start of course because there was some novelty value attached to hiring me; there are autograph hunters even now, many people wanted to ask me about those years, or they wanted to ask me about Archie, about all that had happened. Either way, back then, I was the guy to go to. Poor old Archie. My old mate Archie. He used to call me his troubleshooter and his Mr. Fix-it. His bitch, Albie used to say.

Then came indifference and the selfish heart. You can't fight against that. Experience counts for little these days and all people care about is the fulfilment of their warped desires now. It's all about self-aggrandisement and feathering your own nest with whatever you can forage from the gutter. What a wretched country. I care about my reputation, it's my Achilles heel I suppose. You can't really afford an Achilles heel with legs as dodgy as mine. But there you go, it is what it is, whatever that is. I'm good at what I do, you see? I'm the best at what I do, but we are at the tipping point now and nothing seems to matter any more. It's a free-for-all and I am irrelevant. A one-man show to a row of empty seats, a one-man band to a tone-deaf beggar and a one-man war whose enemy is his own reflection. Christ, that sounds pretentious, doesn't it? Sorry, you must forgive me, I have a background in the entertainment industry as you know, and such things come naturally to us. If you can't forgive me then at least indulge me; we like that even better.

I never thought I would actually end up doing this job. I had played at being a detective when I was a kid. My brother Francis and I used to dress up in our father's trench coat and fedora and we would hunt each other down in the woods behind our house with plastic guns and handcuffs. Sometimes we would tie Mary and Ann from next door to a tree with rope and they seemed to like it. Mary made Francis and me men in that wood and I often find myself wondering what happened to her. She always preferred me, I think. I once beat Francis round the head with a branch and then my mother stopped us playing those games. Those were great days.

Later on I started reading Hammett and Chandler and fell in love with both. I still maintain that you can't get cooler than Chandler. I've struggled for coolness all my life. I could fall in love with coolness above and beyond anything else. I've never had it. I think perhaps I was at my coolest back as a boy in that long trench coat and in that hat that covered my face. That was my zenith of cool. I find that sad. To have actually ended up being a private eye is beyond my wildest dreams, and believe me, that's saying something.

I still find it rather absurd how things have turned this way. Not so long ago, boys were expected to drive trains and girls to stay at home popping out kids and baking bread. How many train drivers does one country need to have? That was when things were simple, or possibly when people were simple. There's nothing wrong with being simple; it's having expectations that crush the soul. Older generations had two choices - black or white, or if you were particularly unfortunate, grey. Having choice broke us, I think. People don't have bosses any more, of course – that's old hat. I suspect there are still a few businesses in the country, someone holding on to their empire, but it must be few and far between. When we were let off the lead, working for the man seemed like a joke fallen flat. Killing the man seemed that much more logical, I suppose. I've yet to actually find out who the man is; someone told me his name was John but I'm really not sure.

Creating the self is the ticket now. Big up the nobodies with the something! Three cheers to the nowhere people with somewhere to go! It's a more acceptable way of feeling unloved, I suppose. At least you get to dress up and pretend you love yourself and it's better than marriage, that much I do know. I got married for marriage and ended up feeling unloved. A man doesn't want to take his home to work with him and I never quite got the two things in flux. My first wife was just waiting for an excuse to leave me. I suppose Albie was too and I gave her excuses aplenty. But in the end, that decision was mine, as she left me no alternative. Does that even count as a decision? She broke my heart, you see. I suppose I'm thankful that after all we'd done there was still something left in me to break, but, you know, grabbing at humanity doesn't dull the pain. I think she will regret the simple life, Albie, because you can't live without a little friction, no, no, NO! Honestly. Believe me. Trust me, I should know; I was a Yes Man for five years.

Before I took this current job, there was a period where I was considering jacking it in. Don't get me wrong I do love being a private eye, but the thrill isn't really there any more. When I started, I felt valued and important, as I was usually hired to track down loved ones and family, friends, people who had been displaced by all that had gone on in the country. I helped love become reacquainted. Can you imagine how great that makes you feel? Of course, that has changed more and more over the months and more often than not now the assignments are nasty and dirty. When consequence fell, people realised that they could lower themselves to the most base emotions and get away with it. From there on the job changed and all I was invariably doing was tracking down enemies so as to make them victims. I have a strict moral and ethical code but I must also eat. It's a horrid hypocrisy that shreds the very best of you.

I suppose it's my own need to rise above what is happening in the country that keeps me at it, whatever the job is and wherever my work leads. It's only been recently that I've really grown to appreciate the need of working. I could be a looter and thief like so many others, but to me I need a reason to get up in the morning beyond survival. I need someone to need me. I guess I have always had a touch of self-loathing and this job keeps me afloat – mentally, if not physically. Without it I would only have my pills to attribute survival to, and how tenuous an existence would that be? These magic little purple pills keep me level, keep the madness at bay – or at least keep me above it, looking in to it at safe distance. The pills keep me sane and this job gives me hope, even amongst the hopeless. It's a wicked contradiction that would make me smile if I could find anything funny about it. Albie made me take them. It was her greatest contribution to my life, she always said.

I argued that her love was of a greater service to my well-being and she laughed. I talk to myself a lot less now I'm on the pills; at least that's what I'm led to believe. I've never told myself the truth of whether I do or not so it's all guesswork on my part, but law of averages would suggest that I'm at least right part of the time, surely?

He phoned and we arranged to meet in a café on the northern border of town. That part of town is about as safe as there is here right now. Murders remain in double figures, and more often than not, what murders there are aren't indiscriminate, there is usually a reason, so provided you haven't pissed on another man's loafers, there is a good chance of getting back out again with your hair in place. It's the only part of town I feel safe venturing into nowadays. Plus, the mere fact that a café keeps in business is a sign that perhaps not all is dead to us. Though if I were being honest if you tasted their tea you would question whether its existence offered anything constructive to society.

It was a Friday late in the month at the start of the year and I pulled in to the car park under a sky that seemed feathered with dirty fat finger streaks. It was a black and white afternoon and tightly trussed up women were outside the café, offering flesh to greedy eyes and hope to selfish hearts. Hearts here are plentiful, but here they beat black, they beat blue, and they beat you over the head if you get too close. He met me outside, his hands buried inside a long trench coat tied up loosely around his ample waist. He reminded me of my dad stood there in that trench coat; maybe even me in some ways. We didn't speak as we went inside. He was paying the bill.

I'd had two mugs of tea before he got to the point. The first had tasted overwhelmingly of washing up liquid and there were orange stains across the mug handle from the previous bean-and-tea combination customer. I complained about it and the haggard creature that worked the till got me a new mug of tea. The second was better, but the mug was chipped at the lip and I had to manoeuvre it away from me whenever I drank. He was on the coffees and were he not anchored down by a barrel chest would probably have been bobbing around at the ceiling. He was matching me two for one and knocked the coffee back like it was water. His consumption of it was extraordinary. He had the sort of demeanour that didn't readily lend itself to inviting friendship. He was a pigeon of a man with delusions of peacock grandeur; a dull cretinous being with a side parting that was never indecisive. In essence, quite pathetic, but instead of allowing himself to fit that role he tried to fight against it, which more than anything irritated long before it ingratiated. The cards, as has been said, were never in his favour. For the purpose of client anonymity I will call him Mr. Pigeon.

'I'd suspected her of having an affair for a while,' he started. 'A husband knows things like that – at least he should. If your missus is banging the baker and you're still buttering the bloomers then you want to take a long hard look at yourself. You get a sixth sense for these things. Different smells, different looks, the length of time she takes in the bathroom. You just know, and if you don't know then you have no business being married.'

'So your wife was having an affair with the baker?'

'Butcher.'

'Oh I see. Well I suppose with a baker's unsociable hours…'

'No, his name was Butcher. He was a plumber. Used to be a plumber.'

'Oh what a cliché. That must have been…'

'It was.'

'I'm not surprised.'

'So I come home and smell his aftershave in the air. The smell carried upstairs. All over the bedroom it was. That smell. Cheap market cologne. Paint stripper with a fancy French name. Anyway, that was my first inkling. She had a bath that night too. Never took baths, my wife. Always a shower woman.'

'Did you ask her about it? What was your first emotion when you found out? Was it anger? Hurt?'

'Curiosity, if I'm being honest.'

'That's strange.'

'Depends where you come from.'

'Was that when you started filming them together?'

'I got that house rigged up tight. Had a cousin worked in surveillance. He got hold of the tiniest damn cameras you ever did see. Incredible what we can achieve nowadays, isn't it?'

I looked out of the window at a corpse lying on the bonnet of a car and decided that he was perhaps only partly right in that statement. Mr. Pigeon finished his coffee. It must have been his sixth, if not his seventh, and made to move back to the till for a refill. This isn't relevant. He returned and burped. I guess that isn't relevant either. I no longer see myself as equipped to understand importance. Though nothing is important, is it? I don't really know what I'm saying anymore. Is that important?

We picked up our conversation again quite easily, as easy as friends, which we most certainly were not.

'I spent the first day watching her in the shower. Watching her dressing, undressing, standing starkers at the mirror checking the fat at the top of her thighs. That was always a big thing for her, I'd tell her she was being paranoid and that she was beautiful but that only seemed to make her more determined that she wasn't. That should have told me something. Butcher came back the second day. He was in a suit. You know, it's funny – well, not so funny, but I actually quite admired him for making the effort.'

'Did you go charging in there?'

'No.'

'Why not?'

'I wanted to see what they did.'

'Was that not…'

'Obvious? Probably. But I was entranced by it. Just watching her. Having that safe distance, that shield, seeing the truth, the real her. I suppose that means nothing to you?'

It didn't. I thought him a sad fool. He was and is and forever will be. That said, I said nothing.

'We were never that adventurous in bed. She'd get paranoid with me behind her and her fat thighs hurt my hips when she was on top. She liked to keep her shirt on and I never took my socks off. I once accidentally hit her in the face with my penis and she screamed. Sorry for saying "penis" to you. I could have substituted the word or left it out but I want to be truthful to the situation as I no longer understand it. That okay?'

'I've heard worse. You know, you really don't need to tell me this.'

'Oh, what's left to be ashamed of? We've come this far.'

'Are you saying you wanted to see what they did in bed? How could you possibly sit and watch that?'

'I don't know. But she was an animal. Up and down, back to front, over and under, straps, whips, leather and lampshades. They ran the gamut of perversity.'

'Lampshades?'

'Do you know what? I think I needed to watch. I needed to see it to try and accept that she was gone and that I could never get her back. Do you understand?'

Lampshades?

'He got so comfortable by the third day that he started walking around in the buff. In my kitchen! Making himself breakfast in my kitchen with everything swinging! They shagged in every room. Against every appliance, the front door, in the shower, on the stairs – it was quite extraordinary. They did things I didn't realise were physically and legally possible. He did fix the leaky tap in the bathroom though, so every cloud...'

'Yet you still want me to find her?'

'I do.'

'Even though you have made peace with never getting her back?'

'I haven't though, don't you see?'

'It's not my job to question the mind.'

'I love her. It was only ever her. I have to find her. I've done what I can but, you know, the way the country is at the moment...'

'I understand.'

'Do you think you will find her?'

'I will try.'

'I suppose I can ask no more than that.'

'Would that we all felt that way.'

We stood and made our way into the car park where we would exchange money. I still like to deal in money.

I'm old fashioned. This is always the hardest part of the job as nowadays, almost without fail, the punters try and beat you down on price. They bitch and moan about the way the country is and try and bleed your pocket. Every punter is a criminal now and I suppose I am too, so sue me. Actually, no, don't. I don't want to have to deal with lawyers any more.

Pigeon gave me all I asked of him and I found myself hating him for it. I was counting the money, safe in the driver's seat of my car, when the café blew up with a hearty bang and Mr. Pigeon landed hard on his face in the middle of car park. Judging by the blood, I would say he was dead as soon as his face hit the gravel. The poor bastard. Two men in expensive suits were chasing a bizarre-looking man waving an envelope through the car park; they had guns and were wearing the finest of silk ties. Pink ties, I believe they were – who wears pink ties? What is the mindset of a man that goes into a shop and selects a pink tie? You know what sort of man that is? It's the sort of man that calls it "salmon" instead of pink. That's what sort of man it is. Either that sort of man or a lawyer. There followed a brief bit of gunplay from two sets of raggedy-arsed back alley bastard people from opposite sides of the car park who probably didn't know who they were shooting at or indeed why they were doing it. I ducked down and waited for it all to pass before starting the car. There seemed little cohesion to their attack; it was instinct rather than anything planned, and they clearly weren't professionals. Amongst the falling remnants of the café, a tabloid newspaper fluttered down from the sky in five different bits. The day's daily tits landed on my windscreen; it was Sandy from Wigan and she was charred and torn but still looked very nice, pretty and almost wholesome, though with breasts like she had you'd never introduce her to your mother. Her theory on the current political crisis unread, I pulled out of the parking space and drove away towards a horizon that looked like a jigsaw puzzle missing the edges. Then came a belch of thunder, and then came screaming, and then finally came the gunshots again.

What was I supposed to do? Admittedly, with Mr. Pigeon dead the job was on shaky ground, but the money was still warm in my hand and when I take a job I see a job through to whatever natural conclusion presents itself. I'm a professional, I'm good at my job and I make no apologies for that. I reasoned the situation out and decided that I would track down the philandering wife and I would tell her about Mr. Pigeon. That seemed a natural point of completion for the job. Besides, the way the market is now, I had no way of knowing if or when I would be employed again so I wanted to see this through; perhaps even try and enjoy it again like I used to at the start. I knew it could be my last job.

I arrived back at the eastern section of the town and drove up and down Apple Avenue twice before settling opposite Mr. Pigeon's house. I don't own binoculars any more as I swapped them for some petrol the other month, but my eyesight is still pretty good despite the hundreds of lonely nights and I was able to cover and reccy without too much hassle. The avenue was decimated but for three houses, his being the most intact. From the outside, his house looked as if what was happening in the country had bypassed it completely. Smoke was coming from a building further up the avenue and small explosions popped in the sky like camera flashes, but other than that it looked quite normal. I decided to allow myself an hour to watch the house before I would head off. Even in the private eye business, you don't really want to be on the streets after dark. I don't dance with the scum anymore, not these days and not with my back.

I decided to enter the house after half an hour's inactivity, more to stretch my legs than anything else; they have been sore for weeks now. I'm so troubled about whatever is afoot with my legs, as I always thought they would be the last to complain such was my vigour in youth. I used to be a fairly proficient long-distance runner back then and I thought I'd put the groundwork in, but clearly not. Whether it has a name or it's just gradual deterioration, there is certainly something there, and if I could find a doctor or a physio

I would ask them but I have no idea whether there are such people any more. I heard a rumour that there was still a florist working in the south of the city so perhaps, if people still want to celebrate or commemorate their love, then there's hope.

The walk to the house was slow and I almost tripped on the kerb. If anyone was watching, it must have looked like I had been drinking again, but I can honestly say that I haven't and for that I'm immensely proud of myself. Booze doesn't mix with my pills and my natural impulses. There is no way I should take that well-travelled road again, no way, that much I do know. Any more alcohol could send me over the edge and I don't want that. The way the country is now, who the hell knows what's over the edge? Almost certainly there aren't any trees.

The inside of the house was very nice, all things considered. It was missing the back wall in the lounge but most other sides were intact and you could almost live there without much of a nod to what was happening. There were paintings framed on the intact wall and the wallpaper was bland but fitting. There was some nice furniture in the lounge, self-assembly was kept to a minimum, but I doubt anything was worth a sneeze in the wind as value would have been stripped out by the looters. A big old arse print, clearly Mr. Pigeon's, was evident on one armchair and the TV didn't work. Everything that was left was very ordered and neat and for that I had to admire the man. The kitchen was stripped of most things, which was no surprise as that is where the money is nowadays, but there were a few tins of food left in one cupboard and a bottle of water on a shelf. I tried to put a family in the house but nothing seemed to fit. I tried to imagine Mr. Pigeon and his wife making a Sunday lunch with kids running around at their ankles but that seemed impossible. It can't have been long ago that such things actually had happened but somehow it felt ridiculous to even assume it now. Much like thinking of dinosaurs, I suppose; I mean, they once walked this earth doing house-sized dumps and eating their friends, but I still can't picture it a reality. Can you? I think I would have been a pterodactyl.

Upstairs, there was damage to the bathroom and the main bedroom. Someone had tried to get the double bed out of the front window and given up and left it when forcing it became too much work. A second TV lay smashed on the bedroom floor, the shattered shards of screen neatly brushed up into two equal piles next to it. The wires of the TV, coming out of the wall, were neatly bound together with a plastic clip. There might have been a fight in the room as there was blood on the carpet, just little bits here and there. A couple of suits were hanging on the back of the door and a balled-up pair of tights was on the floor. There was one shoe by the bedside table. In the en suite, the bath was hanging out of a hole in the wall; a small trickle of water would send it down to the garden. There was tremendous scum. They squeezed their toothpaste from the top. In the main bathroom, a rubber duck sat by the taps of the bath smiling and I took it as a souvenir because I liked the fact that nothing was going to shake that toothy grin and I felt I could do with some inspiration.

I should have left sooner as by the time I turned to the front door, night had come on and I could hear the gunfire and explosions that the darkness always seems to bring these days. I locked the door – which considering the missing lounge wall seemed a little ridiculous, but I guess old habits die hard – and settled in for the night. I had a pack of playing cards and a rubber duck. It was a long night, but better than some I've had recently.

I took position in Mr. Pigeon's armchair to sleep, fitting worryingly well into the arse print and making a mental note to try and think about doing something to change that. I had a fitful sleep full of the predictable bad dreams. The pills were supposed to stop these dreams, they were supposed to level me out and make me approach the human race without a limp, make me normal, make it all better. They had at first, back when I was getting them on prescription and had people telling me what to do, back then they were fine and made it all go away, but now, reliant on the black market trade of pills and potions there is of course the worry that what you are taking may not be what the doctor ordered. I have no idea where my doctor is so I cannot ask him for orders or anything else and I take the pills on trust. They sometimes work. Sometimes they send me so far in to myself that I couldn't find myself to talk to even if I wanted to, other times they make me hallucinate, but more often than not I have a suspicion they do absolutely nothing at all. My son would tell you that such modern drugs were fifty percent action and fifty percent reaction, he would tell you that the illness was perpetuated by myself and that taking the pills is more a way of telling the mind you are helping it and letting it do the work itself rather than actually having any real effect. My son gets by on faith. He doesn't live around here.

I was tied to the armchair in the first dream. Invisible straps held me firm whilst footsteps banged around in the spare bedroom directly above me; someone was turning out cupboards and toppling over furniture. The footsteps seemed to grow in weight, the ceiling above eventually starting to buckle and creak as a fine crack broke through and tiny bits of plasterboard began to rain down. At some unknown time, this ended and my most common dream began. The nights where this dream doesn't play out in some variation or another are few and far between, indeed on the nights that it doesn't come I usually wake feeling confused as if trying to remember the answer to a question I can't remember being asked. It is always a blue house that I am standing in front of, the last house in a row of identical houses and the side of the house is missing, and I am looking in like it were a dolls house. It is raining underneath thunder and the house is swaying slightly. From one top room a weak light is flickering, and then a gunshot and a horrid scream come from deep within the house and I am running to the front door but the front door leads only to another door, and that in turn does the same and I am running straight, through doorways that never end, until finally I barge through a final door and am back out in the road again, staring up at the light as it flickers out and the rain comes down like the coldest stone, born from a tear in the sky. This is the point where I wake and then there is always a quick wash of guilt at the relief that is always evident, always. At least, I think it's that way round.

I woke up lying on the floor of the spare bedroom and turned to look for Albie. I was staring at the rubber duck instead and it made me bawl my eyes out. I shouldn't think about past loves as they are almost always liable to strip away the paper veneer I wrap around my head on a daily basis. I need to be like other men in this world if I'm going to get by, not be like a man. If I had known what would become of this country, perhaps I would have stayed single and fought away love. There is no chain tighter around your neck, pulling you down, than that of the fear for one you love. I miss Albie and I fear for her despite everything. She may have been stronger than me, may have always had a better chance of getting out of the mayhem, but you don't ever stop worrying for someone you love. Love would be a mocking emotion otherwise, wouldn't it? I've seen enough in this job to know that it isn't. Believe me, it really isn't. If you have never been hurt then you only have perfect faith. But if you've never been tested, you've no right declaring total faith in anything.

I should have listened to my mother. She always told me I should never fall in love and certainly never get married, should the two not slip into natural bedfellows. She said women would always use me, "Not for your body Zachary, obviously, but for what you are." I never knew what she meant, but she has a good record at getting it right about me. She laughed when I told her what my new job was. I don't think she believed me; my first wife wouldn't have, that's for sure, though I think that Albie might have believed it. I wish I had lied to my mother. I guess I was kind of proud at the start and that's probably why I told her. "Zachary," she said to me, "my beloved Zachary, my foolish son, listen to me, and listen well. You need a better direction in life. You need to clarify your aims and your aspirations. You need a good pension scheme. You can't be a private dick with a wife and child. Get a proper job." I tried to explain that there wasn't really such a thing as a job any more. I tried to make her understand what had happened to the country, but she's old and her understanding of the modern world got stuck in a groove thirty years ago. I don't want to upset her any more. I know, deep down, that I've always been a disappointment. Truth be told, all she ever really wanted was for me to settle down with an undemanding wife in an uninspiring neighbourhood and circulate unnecessary children with unoriginal names. Unlikely. I could have grown to tolerate it though; I really could. I would have done that for her. For Albie.

The way the country is now, it's hardly conducive to stable relationships. This job certainly isn't and I always knew that, and it's a shame because I could have been conventional given a chance or half a mind. My first wife was never at home and whatever we had that was conventional never really made it past the birth of our son. Instead of bringing us closer together, it moved us apart. Maybe it was the responsibility, maybe we were too young to be playing at adults, and maybe it was just what was meant to be for us, I don't know. We were lodgers who would greet with perfunctory pleasantries, we were kids ourselves, children who made an adult mistake and just wanted to be old enough to move on. Despite all that, I do still think it would be nice to come home to someone, to have someone there no matter what, that I could look at and talk to. It would be nice to make grand the mundane and I guess you can only do that with a loved one, lest you talk about the weather, and of course, nowadays, that's not a wide topic. I have often thought that if we were more satisfied with the mundane, we may have sidestepped the trouble. Though who am I to have answers to anything? I'm nothing any more. I wish I had known years ago the absolute joy in that position.

I would have liked a family business; I can certainly see the appeal in that. Even if I could afford it, my son wouldn't ever come in with me, though, no way – he's too busy trying to save the world. He wears sandals and doesn't believe in deodorant. He doesn't believe in deodorant! He said that once he's saved the world he's going to become a missionary. I told him that would be ironic as that was the only position his mother would let me have sex with her in. We haven't spoken since then. I guess he must be busy, what with saving the world. I tried to tell him it was pointless but he seems pretty determined. He's working from the rainforests down, and I told him he had it all back to front, said he should save the people first and then work up. It doesn't matter what part of the planet you save if you are leaving people around dumb enough to come in after you and mess up all your hard work. "It's always people, son," I said to him the last time we spoke, "that's what will fail us all in the end." He didn't understand. The first time Albie met him, she said he was an idealist. I said there was nothing remotely ideal about the whole sorry shindig.

Women never seem to linger. Albie was the longest

by a mile, which doesn't say much. Actually, it says quite a lot, doesn't it? I like to think it's just my social deficiencies that sends them packing and not anything to do with my manly prowess. A man doesn't like to think that. It's not like I never had my fair share of women; I mean, I started my career in kids' TV so as you can imagine I have had dalliances about as debauched as you can get. All sorts. Then I met Albie and it all changed. I knew she was the one. Not just one of the ones, but the one. I knew we were going to be a pair.

I found a stash of food under a floorboard in the spare room. It was neatly bundled up in a linen bag and tied with rope. A few tins of beans – some had sausages in – a packet of biscuits, flasks of water, a bottle of Scotch and some packets of fizzy sweets minus the fizz. Hardly the healthiest of midnight feasts, but food is food and you learn not to get picky these days. I remember, as a boy, being delirious with joy whenever we had beans with sausages in for tea. To this adult mouth they tasted absolutely vile. There is, of course, a whole stack of adult disappointments, but that is very near the top of the list.

I hadn't expected to find any clues in their old house – there wasn't much there that indicated a life lived – but I like to get a feel for my clients. I used to know a detective many years ago and he said he used to do something similar; he said that there was much to be gleaned from spending time at the victims' place of dwelling and piecing together their life, by that which was important to them. He said you could tell a lot about someone just by what they had out on their shelves, by looking at what they deemed worthy of show you could, if you were astute enough, know all that was pertinent to that person's life. Here of course, in chez Pigeon, in the current climate, it was like trying to guess a portrait with the face rubbed out. I still like to do it, though. I'm thorough.

I was preparing to leave, ready to move out to try and catch the tail of Mr. Butcher the plumber, when I chanced a look out of the window in the master bedroom and saw the body of an old lady on the steps to a house opposite. No great surprise, of course – I'm sure you've seen similar – but at that moment, in that frame, there was something utterly repugnant about the whole thing that froze my blood and held me in the window like a broken mannequin. There were smiling children playing next to it, joyful screaming brought from plastic guns and the freedom of this day and every other. I thought of Francis and I as children, and Mary and Ann and their willing companionship, all of us playing out our games together in the deep dark woods. Then, as now, everyone killed each other ten times over and got back up and did it all over again. The immortal children. There was something about that contrast; young and old, decay and youth that repulsed a fascination out of me and I couldn't look away. It's harder these days to pinpoint children's ages, I find; I suppose these were just shy of teenage trouble, that impossible grey area where people aren't sure whether to delight or fear. I watched until they tired of whatever game they had invented and, bonded by friendship or acquaintance, sauntered off to create anew, leaving the old to drain away into the ash-grey morning that never once promised respite or release. I took it as my cue to leave. I have always feared children, and here, plastic gun or not, all I had to defend myself with was a rubber duck.

In the job of the private eye, there are a few givens that you must adhere to if you are to have success; you don't get close to the wallet or the target, you can't afford facial expressions, keep vices small, always carry clean clothes in your car, condoms in your wallet and detachment in your heart. Never assume that you have achieved your goal until you have turned your back on the gig and never, ever, under any circumstances, leave a phone ringing – it's just not good business sense. The sound of a ringing phone does something to me, something magical; my body suddenly aligns with my mind at the sound of a phone. I don't know why, I have no intelligent people to ask if it means anything, beyond a professional outlook to my work, but it feels like it does. Pigeon's phone started to ring as I was halfway down the stairs and the sound was muffled and flat but my senses still came alive at the sound. I searched for it, all around the hall I paced, looking in the other downstairs rooms, all the time wondering if I was imagining it, imaging that I was willing it to ring. The sound seemed to fade to a whisper, but as I turned back to the stairs again it started to ring louder, demanding, incessant; it had to be heard. I followed the noise to a cupboard under the stairs, to an old and battered phone unit and a receiver snapped in two. I grabbed it and the ringing stopped. Ready to berate my own ineptitude, perhaps to break the phone again, I was about to give up when the answer machine suddenly kicked in and grabbed the call; a broken voice made the greeting and I gently picked the unit up and took it out of the cupboard and into my arms. The call cut off and I was about to place the phone back when I noticed the machine displaying ten unplayed messages; a small and gently red light clicking on and off, winking at me with suggestion. I sat on the bottom of the stairs and played the tape back. Each message carried the same voice; a tired and emotional voice coming in short gobbles between stutters and moans, a woman's voice – Mrs. Pigeon's voice. I had pictured her, since her husband's tale in the café, as perhaps we all would a cheat, but here, rendered impersonal by the machine, she sounded hollow and weak and I couldn't fit my imagination of her with the distant reality. The messages started with contrition and developed, through hostility, to all-out pleading.

'Where are you? I need to know that you're safe. I've been stupid. I love you!'

She loved him, she said. She was stupid, she said. Can they make another go of it? I broke down in tears as the image of Mr. Pigeon lying on the gravel car park of the café came back to my mind. I didn't know what to do, or say, even though I was obliged to do neither. I merely, as is instinct in my job, took my Dictaphone from my jacket pocket and recorded the messages on to it, staring down at the phone like a guilty man looking down at a felled foe. I put the phone back and left the house, slumping into my car and breaking into uncontrollable fits of sobbing against the steering wheel. I cried myself limp, I was drained, my nose was starting to bleed and the drops were flecking my shirt. I necked some pills, probably too many, and soon slipped into automatic. Everything slowed, the scenery in front of me shed the sharp edges and I felt like I was in a cartoon. Everything was soft and comfortable. I moved the car into first and trundled away, travelling on instinct towards whatever fell into my path. I had to see her, had to finish my job. I couldn't shake the feeling that somehow this would be the last job of this kind, that never again would I be needed by my punters and that this was it, the last adventure. My phone doesn't ring so much these days.

I think I need to get some promotion if I'm really going to make a go of things. I need to get the word out there, utilise my face and use the recognition... TV, radio, the

Internet... It's been proved that if you want a tedious or grotesque act performing, nine out of ten people would choose a minor celebrity to perform it. So it would be daft of me not to use the advantage I have. The Internet is the big thing now, has been for years of course, but now that so many people don't leave the house anymore, it's become a lifeline, a crutch, their link to the rest of the world should they ever be so desperate for company. I fought against the Internet for years. You know that no one has written me a letter in three years? Generation after generation of bad handwriting, that's what will happen. In a couple of generations' time, if we make it that far, and I am more often than not an optimist, I reckon kids won't even know how to hold a pen. The pen will still be mightier than the sword, of course, but you will always be able to destroy the world with the push of a button. But far be it for me to bite the hand that is going to feed; it has its advantages and, getting my mug on board, it will be priceless. Thank the Lord for the shallow end of the gene pool and their elevation of celebrity to the plane of the mythical. They made me, they made Albie and they made Archie. They have let us get away with so much. Hedonism is an art form. Am I wrong to take advantage?

This job makes sense to me. It's the fabled black and white clarity of purpose my old folks banged on about. Sure they meant office work, but the principles are the same. I'm going to buy a nice house again when the business picks up; yeah, a nice big house. Get straight, get normal, and perhaps get a swimming pool like Albie always wanted. She might even be proud of me. So I'm going to record a little ad for the Internet. It makes me feel a little cheap even at my competitive prices. I feel a bit like a whore. But needs must. If I hadn't been who I had been, and had the public not... Well, you know... I'm merely a product now, you see? Everyone is a product or a commodity, a killer or a corpse. We all have a price now, even in a free-for-all, all of us hanging on to establish our worth. I've always got the TV presenting to fall back on if things don't work out. It may be the end of the world, or the start of the next one, but we will always have TV.

There were three plumbing businesses this side of town and I got lucky on the first. Laker & Butcher Plumbing Services was set in the middle of a large industrial estate further up town, a part of town where the dead have beds and the women were classier, the tricks dearer; a small cluster of portakabins with a lopsided sign was all it was, they were never set for world domination it seemed. Butcher had been with them for years, starting as apprentice and working his way up to joint partner. He was the go-to man if the facts were to be believed, but his record seemed to stop about five years ago; he had left his name on the notepaper but whether he still worked there was unclear. Laker was an old man and was supposed to be taking it easy these days, playing golf and staring at bushes in his garden. I hadn't considered how recent events must have pissed off the newly retired. It must be hard, working all your life to afford yourself a relaxing retirement and then the country breaks and everyone starts killing each other. I suspect people still play golf, though, so maybe he's not too narked. Most of the portakabins were wrecked and looted of equipment; one remained intact and served as an office, spilling forth as much information as I needed. The floor was a carpet of invoices and folders, dots of blood were fairly spread around amongst them, a tooth sat on a blue folder – beaten out, one would suspect. There were a couple of photos framed on the wall, plumbers holding certificates and fake smiles. One such plumber held a golden plastic wrench mounted on a cheap base, some award for something or other that meant nothing to anyone any more. I wondered which was Butcher. I settled on a thin-looking chap with greasy hair and a crooked smile. I needed a face and his would do as well as any of the others.

I took a moment to rest my legs, gently massaging the thighs and rolling my ankles anti-clockwise, listening to the tiny clicks and snaps and wincing as it sent little jagged flares of pain upwards. I could feel the pills kicking in and punching through the blackness and I closed my eyes until my head emptied. My legs were on fire, throbbing and dancing under me, my muscles twitching in little spasms. I rolled my head and scrunched up my shoulders until everything settled back into place and I could open my eyes again. I stood, crossed to the front wall and stared through a hole and out in to the street. It was unnaturally quiet. The sun looked bloody and the sky deathly calm, like a burning hole in a landscape painting. A gentle breeze blew at the rubble-strewn pavements of the industrial estate and small dust clouds formed and broke, litter tumbled slowly, and through the hole in the wall came a whistling as sharp as a knife. I took Butcher's address from the employee's records and left.

I kept seeing Pigeon's face in everything – in buildings and bushes, on the pavement, in the sky; inanimate objects coming together to form his features. I could hear his voice on the edges of my ears, I could feel the love he still had for his wife, that horrid aching and yearning like a heaven guarded by a wall too high to scale. Then I was piecing together her voice from the Dictaphone, trying to find something, a clue, a hint, and a sign that somehow she could make everything better. I wanted to hate her, I wanted her not to care and take my news with a shrug of the shoulders and a hollow smile, but every word she spoke dragged me into my shoes a little further.

'You see, it was never that I didn't love you. You must understand that. When everything changed, I was so scared; it was circumstance... That sounds so trite. Yes, it was

infatuation too. But infatuation was all it was. It was never love. It was only ever you that could bring love from me. That scared me too…'

I eased the car under fifty as the town fell low behind me and the empty horizon filled up the windscreen. There is safety in loneliness but it didn't stop my eyes darting back and forth across the road, waiting for surprise or attack. You soon learn to accept that if a bullet comes then chances are there is not much you can do about it, and if you are ever to leave the house again, you take your balls in your own hands and try not to get too itchy a finger. The alternative is staying at home with nothing but my own company to keep me going and I know I wouldn't get far on that.

It was twenty miles to Butcher's home and I would need to fill up the tank if I were to make it. This brings its own problems, of course, as I'm sure you know yourself. When the country imploded there were a few with an entrepreneurial bent who took the chance to quickly hoard up that which we all viewed as vital; food, clean water, beautiful people and petrol. There is a burgeoning market for each and each comes at a price above its worth. There are still a few areas that trade in money but more often than not it's the practical that people want. There are some who believe that the country will survive and are saving up money ready for the day, most however want things to make survival that much easier. As for petrol, well, usually on most A-roads there are several petrol points where makeshift people in tumbledown shacks offer cans of petrol for as much as they think they can get from you. They always come in twos, one to trade and one to threaten with whatever weaponry they have. This enterprise often brings shysters out to play and you need to be careful; you should never fill up your car without your own weapon to hand. I never used to advocate the carrying of weapons but now I have no choice. I have a trusty pistol taped underneath my dashboard, but have only had cause to fire it once. I say that like it's something to be proud of. The day of that first bullet is one I don't wish to repeat but, like graffiti on the brain, the memory fades but never leaves. Nor, I suppose, should it, as I need to retain some humanity no matter how paltry. They will not have me. Even if they saw something worth having, they will never have it. Not from me.

I've only ever been done over by a petrol thief once but it was enough to knock my back out of kilter and things have never been the same since. They were young kids and I should have known better – a man of my age. Truth was I think they did it more because they recognised me than for money. Guilty by association, I presume; either that or they actually were confusing me with Archie. He's the one that got the most flak, of course. I often wonder whether he's still alive. It must be impossible for him to even set foot in the real world now. I hope he's okay. You don't stop caring for a friend, no matter what they do. I've made enough mistakes in my life to know not to judge.

The lawyers shafted Archie. The lawyers screwed us all. I probably shouldn't tell you that, there's probably a law against it, but it's true. It was the lawyers, the eminent firm of Schuttler & Wise, which turned me out of my last job, that destroyed Archie and made Albie leave. Those nasty little vermin. They say every generation creates the enemies they deserve. When I was growing up, it was estate agents; it's cyclical I suppose. I miss that job, I miss having that purpose. Archie wouldn't have sacked me if it had been anything to do with him, and he was so apologetic about it. I suppose after what happened it was inevitable that the lawyers would pounce and take over. They were always there in the shadows, anyway; it was like protective parents watching their children in the school pantomime, hiding in the wings waiting to pounce if you fluffed your lines or pissed your pants. They are running the whole show now. Archie was always just a mouthpiece, but he really did want to do well, you know? You should know that. You should believe that. He was so enthusiastic. I know we made mistakes, but what did you expect?

What happened to us all? When did people start having opinions? Stop being docile and subservient? It should have been kept a rich man's pursuit, this country;

it should have stayed distant and unobtainable, like Archie always used to say, it should have stayed in the hands of the "unreachable, untouchable, unrelenting stone figureheads," because such an impenetrable detachment would have kept people suffocated and quiet like it always used to. People would have accepted their worthless, fragile limitations like the good old days and perhaps we would have avoided all of this. We are on our own now until they tip this country upright again. No laws. No rules. Nothing. We make our own path now that there is no one in charge. We have to, don't we? Just us humans and what we do. I'm no different, I just used to be on the telly. I do try and accentuate the positive, though. Even in this situation, it's like my mother always used to say, "A change is as good as a rest, Zachary; familiarity breeds chickens."

I pulled in to the McCracken sister's petrol shack five miles outside of town, I'd been there before and they had been as pleasant as pleasant got now that no one is pleasant anymore. Two old birds with greasy hair and doughy limbs, usually matching dresses cut straight from the curtains of a seventies sitcom, and horrid wooden jewellery crafted by tasteless hands. Various weaponry was usually slung over, tucked under or strapped to one or the other of them depending on who won the coin toss that morning. I once saw them shoot a burly man in a tracksuit who tried to pinch a canister from them; just one quick rifle shot to the back is all it took, and as the man tumbled to the ground the other sister sprang forward and expertly caught the petrol canister before anything was spilt and methodically put it back amongst their stock. I saw no enjoyment from them, just a simple cold practicality in their eyes. It was such casualness in evil deeds that terrified me about the country but yet, perversely, also gave me the greatest hope for its recovery.

I gave them my watch and they gave me a canister and a half of petrol. Hardly a fair swap in terms of monetary value, but I reasoned out that where we currently stand, the means to get away from it is far more vital than marking the time spent there. The sky is either light or dark. You fill the hours in between the best way you can. I emptied the half-full canister into the tank and was storing the other in the boot when a strange-looking chap approached us at a quick hobble from out of the diseased trees opposite the McCracken's shack. He was muddied and bruised, his clothes torn and hanging limply like a scarecrow's dress-down day attire. He tried a smile but it fell off his face. The armed sister swung a shotgun towards him and shouted a warning and he stopped still in the road with dancing legs and poor man's jazz hands on the end of raised arms. He gibbered crazily, nonsensical garbage; he asked me for a lift and I asked him where he was going. "Anywhere," he said. I agreed to take him there.

His name was Edgerton and he wouldn't stop talking. He rambled on in great, enthused tones, his arms and hands punctuating or elaborating every sentence or anecdote. He was the sort of bore that sits in the corner at parties drinking your booze and telling you how shit your house is and yet refuses to leave. He smelt of a sewer and it was with a heavy heart and light pocket I realised that the leather upholstery would probably need cleaning once he'd left. I try to like people regardless of the myriad reasons they usually put forward for making that difficult; Edgerton, however, was going to be hard work.

'You have no idea the journey I have been on, Zach. No idea.'

'Or interest,' I mumbled into my chin.

'I saw them going into the café toilets with the briefcase. They were bug-eyed men with no time in their eyes. I knew the smell of their skin lotions and recognised their socks. They may as well have had a neon sign on their foreheads saying "lawyer", you know? Of course you know. They have been on my back for longer than I can remember. I thought I would be safe there; I thought we would all be safe. They thought I hadn't seen them. I got out of the café before it exploded, just, the window blew out into my face and I tripped, broke something in my hand but I ran, I got away from there – from them.'

'This a café in the north of the town?'

'Yeah. You were there, I know, I saw you.'

'Small world.'

'I certainly hope not. I'm banking on there being a lot more out there somewhere.'

'We're in deep trouble if there isn't.'

'I quite agree.'

'Is this just a coincidence?'

'I hope not. I came to the café to find you.'

'Why?'

'Because I wanted to see you.'

'Why?'

'Because I needed to find you.'

'Why did they want to kill you?'

'I know something they don't want me to know.'

'What's that?'

'I'm in possession of information that could change the world.'

'What would that be?'

'It's in an envelope, he wrote it down for me.'

'Who did?'

'The man. The main man. He came to me and called himself John.'

'Someone told me the man was called John. I didn't believe them.'

'It's the name he's using at the moment. He's incognito.'

'Are we talking about a different man?'

'I have no idea. Are you talking literally or metaphorically?'

'I have no idea.'

'Are you religious, Zach?'

'I'm an atheist.'

'That's a shame. Are you sure?'

'That's the one where you aren't sure, isn't it?'

'You are thinking of agnostic, it isn't really relevant.'

'Why ask then?'

'Just making small talk.'

'Don't feel the need.'

So it went on and on, with Edgerton talking in cryptic code about whatever had got him so excited and had over-inflated his opinions. We passed two small shattered ghost villages and, after entering a third, pulled over and watched fresh flames eating away at a gazebo whilst we ate a small lunch from Pigeon's stored rations. Edgerton started playing with the envelope, turning it over in his dirty hands and wafting it at the air and then at me, expecting, I expect, me to grab it and greedily consume whatever information was in it. Clearly he expected me to care. I tried to but was found wanting. Once you have been on TV, the novelty of freaks wanting to see you soon disintegrates. I shouldn't complain, because were it not for the unbalanced TV-watching-celebrity-obsessing morons that stalk with pen or gun then there was no way I'd ever have got where I had got. Though, of course, on the flipside I'd never have fallen so far either. So, fuck them. Fuckers.

'I know who you are, you know?'

'Many do.'

'I knew Archie. I was quite important to him.'

'Good.'

'I used to watch that kids' programme you did on a Saturday. They don't make them like that anymore.'

'Thanks.'

'I don't blame you for what happened.'

'That's big of you. I don't blame myself either.'

'Or Archie.'

'Yeah.'

'You should take the envelope. I was told to spread the word. Truth is, I have had it for a long time and have had no idea what to do with it. He said I'd know when I met the right person. Of course, that should have been Archie and it nearly was. But here I am with you. I think you are my last chance, Zach.'

'No pressure, then?'

'Don't you want to change the world?'

'I told you I wasn't religious. If it's a religion that needs selling then I'm not buying on principal. Warm tea and regular bowel movements is all it takes to get me to sing halleluiah. Could be I'm a man with too simple an outlook for your merry meandering. Perhaps you should go pick it up with someone with a larger forehead.'

'Don't you want to make this country better again?'

'What makes you think I could do that?'

'You're a celebrity, you can do anything. It's the one word key to all jobs. The answer to everything.

This world gives you anything if you're famous.'

'That time is past. Don't you think?'

'Is it? There is a generation out there that grew up watching you on television, Zach. There is a bond of trust that grows out of that. You talk and people will listen. Look what happened with Archie. Did not rather too many people listen to him? I'm nothing; no one will listen if I speak, and no one will care. I'm not famous, I'm not important. People would write me off as a crank and ignore it. I've been on a spiritual journey through this broken country, up and down the land, people after me at every turn, people desperate to stop me passing this on to another. People that would think nothing of blowing up a mini-market or café of innocent people to stop me and I've reached the end of this particular journey Zach. I can't run anymore. I won't. You take the envelope, you spread the word. It couldn't be Archie, I tried Albie, but now you are all I have left. Perhaps it should have always been you, Zach.'

'You've seen Albie?'

'Yes. We spoke. She thought me a fool, I believe.'

'You've seen her? When?'

'Time gets confusing. Days, probably weeks, certainly not months.'

'But... Is she...'

I wasn't actually sure what I was going to ask him, probably I was asking him to confirm she was alive, maybe I was going to ask if she spoke about me, perhaps that, but probably not. Truth is, I don't know. Gunfire stopped my question anyway, and as soon as the bullet struck Edgerton in his chest, whatever my question was going to be at that point was moot. I like to think that I was going to ask if she was safe.

Why do I still feel guilt about everything that happened? She never felt guilt. Why can't I be like Albie? At least I'm not selfish. That's what I should have said to her. As last lines go, it's better than "have a nice day." I knew she was going to do it, so I made sure I did it first. It was the gentlemanly thing to do, even though leaving her tore me open and folded my inside out. It near killed me. But she left me no choice. That she would have done it anyway is no real comfort. I love her, but they made it impossible. I didn't even get to walk off into the sunset. It was pissing down that day. I hated Albie when I first met her and I think the feeling was mutual. I'm surprised we even got past a cordial greeting to be honest. I had pulled a seven-day shift linking the kids' programmes one half term and was getting by on a mix of ketamine, cocaine and cola bottles, you know, the chewy ones? I was counting the cracks in the ceiling one lunchtime in the studio canteen when she comes over and takes a seat opposite me. She was on the seeded fruit diet and was crazy-eyed. We introduced ourselves. She said she had heard of me, I apologised for not being able to return the favour. She said she was a nobody. She was a nobody. Back then she was nothing. She was waiting to go into a recording of a quiz show. It was her fifth quiz show that year and she'd already won a hamper and a caravan. She said she was doing it for her dad, whatever that meant – I really didn't care because she was beautiful, and obviously when faced with beauty, reason is redundant. I told her she should be on TV, properly so, presenting or something like that, but she said she had no discernable talent and I had to fight to convince her. I didn't bother telling her that talent wasn't necessarily the yardstick; I figured she'd get there eventually.

At the start, when she was a nobody, there was something about her wide-eyed childishness that was endearing. I do like seeing people at the bottom of the heap, yet to be diluted by bitter cynicism, it's always a glow for the heart and soul. Optimism and hunger, well, someone's got to have it, haven't they? But when the cynicism does come…

"Love isn't reason enough anymore. That's all I'm saying. Love is not a reason to stay with you, Zachary. Plus I don't love you anymore." There you go, a planned lifetime condensed into two lines. That was all I was worth. Two lines, a footnote – an aside. Then I hit her with the original one-two of what she had done and she just stared at me amazed and riddled with the disease of shame. I shouldn't have enjoyed that moment, but I did. She packed a bag and she left. I called to her when she was at the garden gate but she didn't hear me. I often wonder what would have happened if she had. Maybe something, probably nothing. I don't know where it all went wrong, I loved her, cared for her, cherished her, supported her and gave a shoulder when it was needed, we were great and we had legs. That's all you need in a marriage; legs and shoulders. Admittedly you also need a heart to be happy, but we had all we needed to make it functional, but even with that she managed to make a mess of it.

She said she would love me forever. I never thought she would change her mind. They say it's a female prerogative, but she wasn't like that; I wouldn't have turned my heart over to any old woman, you know? I think I knew from the start, if not that day in the canteen then at least when I got her her first TV gig. Love at first sight is merely justification from the desperate and the foolhardy, so I don't know what it was with Albie. Lust at first sight? Probably. It's a human trait as ingrained as a selfish heart; you walk down any street in any country in any world and it is nought but a meat market. We are all buying, we are all selling, eyes on each other, sometimes quick and sometimes lingering but always sorting and filing the beauty from the blunders, the art from the tacky, the willing from the unobtainable. With Albie and I it was no different, and that love would come along to describe that horrid empty and hungry feeling we had was as much of a surprise to her as it was to me. "We should do something about this," she said. So we did.

She started as the runner on my Saturday morning show. She was at my command and she did everything for me. Then, of course, when we got together it was a daily struggle to keep her interested. She was promoted to operating the hand puppet Mr. Chuff that the editor wanted me to interact with during the viewer's letters section. I think talking to that was what sent me mad and prompted a lifetime on pills. At least I don't think it was just life, women and alcohol; there had to be more to it than that. Mr. Chuff was this hairy little monstrosity that Dave on camera 3's wife made, an ugly thing with a rubber tongue and the ping-pong ball eyes of a dictator. Well, I don't need to tell you, do I? Three album recording artist with four number ones! Who knew? Albie was great at it, the editor always used to say she "gave great chuff" and who was I to argue? It was true to say she gave him an earthy quality that a pound of black wool over a latex glove had no right to have, and she had talent for it certainly. But she also had an ego and an appetite to quench the thirst that ego always prompted "Take me here, Zach." She would always say, "let's go to this party!" "Introduce me to this person," "that person," "Every damn one!" She'd have gone to the opening of an artery if someone were taking pictures. We did a photo shoot for one of those tatty rags that go to die in dentist's waiting rooms, "Zach and

Albie welcome us into their new home!" the headline said. The home wasn't new and I personally didn't welcome them, but, there you go, we all lie. You have to lie in that business. I have always been wonderful at it. I have a variety of facial expressions for every conceivable situation; I can ingratiate, appease, charm and I can look like I care. My face was my weapon. Despite what my mother would tell you, I was TV handsome to a tee. You probably remember. I used to have my face insured for five hundred thousand pounds. Every time I got in a bar fight, ten men in suits would hold their breath and whistle a one-note requiem out of their ring pieces. There was a period when I was trying to crack prime time that I slept in an astronaut's helmet. Albie gave me a love bite once and it took me a month to convince my agent that I didn't want to sue. It was a crazy time. We didn't sue people back then, do you remember that? I do. When did that change? When did people start selling the ability to sue? Was it just the lawyers? Is that the moment they made their pitch for world domination?

I struggle to remember how long ago it was I last saw Albie. Time is confusing – Edgerton was right about that at least. It was just before Archie gave his speech and things began to change. I have no idea how long ago that was; perhaps you do. It's funny how quickly everyone has settled into this new groove. I suppose, deep down, we are all bred for anarchy, so perhaps it should be no surprise so many have taken to it with such ease. They say you can't extract that which has never been there in the first place, and so those that relied on human decency for their dose of optimism were the ones that fell hardest. I always saw it differently; I always felt that in a time where anything was possible, so must be any emotion. We all have these emotions within us, to cheat, to screw, to lie and to kill. It was, at least I believe, only guilt that kept us suppressed and guilt came from having consequences, so it stands to reason that if you take that away…

Three men were charging out of the smoke of the burning gazebo, guns aloft, firing indiscriminately, hollering and screaming with delight. Edgerton fell backwards, his chest bloodied, his face confused. I managed to dive back in to the open car window before the second wave of bullets came and my dear old car took the brunt. I turned the engine over at the second attempt and shifted her in to first. A bullet pinged off the wing mirror and another punched through the top of the windscreen breaking it down onto the dashboard and seats like a glass waterfall. I could see that my right hand was cut and as I leant my weight down on to the accelerator I started touching myself in important areas looking for a wound. I couldn't feel anything, but that's nothing new. The back window fell in and another bullet bedded into the headrest of the passenger seat, another hit the dash and broke the air conditioning. I moved through the gears, my body bent forward, my forehead against the wheel and I floored the accelerator, swerving across the country road, mounting the edge and regaining the road just enough to pull out of range.

The envelope was stuck to the bonnet, one end plastered in thick blood, the other wedged under the one working windscreen wiper. Despite the speed, indifferent to its puny weight against the force of the wind battering it, it remained still, hugging the car like it was painted on. I pulled off the road after a mile and entered a small coppice, guiding the car along a small bendy gravel road and nestling it between two puny trees before cutting the engine and stepping out. The shelter and disguise were not enough should anyone pass, but it was the best that was on offer and, as I have learned, a token effort is better than no effort at all. If we all made token efforts each day, we might just get ourselves back to where we were, or not – I don't know, who am I to know? I brushed the shards of glass from the seats and prised the envelope off the bonnet and stared at it. Looking at the sealed mouth it seemed to be smiling at me; a mischievous bloody grin. It repelled me and I wanted to flick it away, but I couldn't. There was something beyond curiosity that prevented me, something creeping and defining that seemed to emanate from it like it were a pulsing heart. As much as there was intrigue, there was also an immense dislike of Edgerton and that had the high-end cards; hatred is a disease and it's catching. I pocketed the envelope, returned to the car and took out the last of Pigeon's rations. I would have killed for a cup of tea. No, killed isn't the right word; I hadn't yet sunk to that level. I would have maimed for a cuppa, almost definitely.

Chewing limp biscuits down my dry throat, I wandered through the coppice and out into a thicker patch of trees, most diseased but some still fighting the fight, and across to an old picnic area where a small square of benches sat on a small square of concrete in front of a small square bin and a long rectangular hut which once housed an ice cream parlour and café. Someone had written on the sidewall "WATCH THAT CHILD!" A child had written "FUCK OFF" underneath, or it might have been a childish adult, or perhaps someone trapped in between, but either way it was written in blood and the chilling effect would be no more diluted whatever the hand. Walking on through piles of rubbish, I saw a small charred circle on a patch of grass and the embers of a campfire. The grass was flattened on either side into vague human shapes and several discarded condoms, shrivelled and pathetic, were dotted around like sad trophies from one last winning night. The door to the hut was swinging lazily on rusted hinges and easing out a tired yawning sound like bed springs under obligatory sex. I wandered in, holding an arm to my nose to shut out the stench of all bad things that seemed to be pumping out from inside.

The hut was stripped to the wood it was standing up in, and even that showed signs of letting go. Insects roamed the walls with a lazy speed, cobwebs hugging each corner and curve. As I walked, the floor sighed and snapped underneath me like kindling under a weak flame. The ice cream parlour stank of milk so far turned it was looking for the udder. Smiling cartoon pictures on the menu stared out through dirt patches and blood smears. Some photos were dotted around the till; pictures of smiling families at the picnic tables, and sunny children gobbling down massive ice creams. Moving on into the café, another smell mixed in and turned the milk away. It was the smell of death. Our country's personal perfume.

The café, like the ice cream parlour, was stripped bare. The meagre light coming in was like police flashlights probing a crime scene, although what greeted me was no crime – at least not in the literal sense. A young couple, that was what I liked to think they were, were hung from the eaves by a car towrope, rocking gently from side to side. Her right hand was tied to his left by an elastic band and their hands were interlocked, whether through rigor mortis or will it was impossible to say. I wandered the room looking for a note, looking for a clue as to who they might have been, as is forever my instinct, but nothing was there. Perhaps there never was anything, perhaps there was no one they cared enough about to tell, though should people really need to explain such a decision these days? I like to think that for each of them, the only person that mattered enough to tell was holding their hand as they passed over and that that itself, for him and for her, was all they needed.

I could feel tears again and left, stumbled out of the café and tripped on the bottom step, spilling forward and landing in a heap on the grass. I felt disorientated for a second and sat at one of the benches to steady myself. I searched for my pills and crunched two down, letting the inevitable come on and kick back. I let my head drain away and my focus return. Should I have buried them? I have asked myself that question a few times and have yet to find the answer, or at least an answer that doesn't mark me a bastard or coward. In my job, you can't invest in emotions too readily. You just can't. I'm sorry. For me, right then and even more now, I could invest only in the matter at hand, and that was locating Mrs. Pigeon and relaying the news about her husband. Being messenger was bad enough, must I play gravedigger too?

'To be honest, from where we came from to where we got always seemed a miracle to me. I know I wouldn't have done it without you, and I hope you feel the same. I've always been independent of mind and soul, my failing people would tell you, but you changed all that. You made me strong. Did I not do the same for you? They say love conquers all. Now I don't believe that any more than you do, but surely it can

conquer this, can't it? If not, what hope is there left to invest in?'

I listened to the messages on the Dictaphone again, straining for something between the words, wanting so much for my job to be eased by a tone of indifference from that little mechanical voice. I knew it was never going to come, no matter how many times I played the phone messages back. I played them back again anyway.

There had been gunshots close by for five minutes or so (well, a lot longer of course, if you're going to be picky) but the gunshot that yanked me from my immersion in the Dictaphone tape seemed to come from over my shoulder, a sharp crack beyond the dead trees behind the hut. My senses flooded back over my dusty brain and drained downwards, like the first hung-over piss of the morning. I pocketed the Dictaphone and scampered back to the car for my pistol, each step too heavy for my legs and each flare of pain making me feel my body rested on bags of hot coals. I fumbled the pistol and it fell with a small thud on to the grass. I picked it up and tried to slip it in to my belt but it missed and hit the ground again. I picked it up a second time and something pinged in my back and I had to stifle a scream as I straightened. I decided this time to keep the pistol in my grip as I ran, hobbled and eventually stumbled back to the hut and peered through the withered branches towards the sound of the gunfire.

At first, I could see nothing. The drab blanket the trees cast over everything stifled colours and definition and was prepared to reveal nothing beyond the wispy cream sky that poked between the vicious-looking branches, a sky that seemed drained, waiting patiently for nightfall and respite from scrutiny. I stepped to the trees, careful not to step on fallen branches or trip over rabbit holes. How I dearly wished to see a rabbit. They do still exist, apparently. Though I'm taking that on trust. A few feet in, the trees started to thin out even more and the land beyond fell in to view, bit by bit, rising up under the cold sky and slowly wrapping itself around the edges of my vision. I rested against the last tree that looked strong enough to take my weight and peered out across a patch of farmland.

At first, I saw nothing that seemed out of place. I didn't question why there were five scarecrows positioned in a line in the middle of the field, there was no reason to question the need of five, nor even in the absence of birds nowadays did I even consider questioning the need of one. Two men stood about twenty feet away from them, loading rifles. I looked into the sky, hopeful of seeing birds again, tempted even in my childish enthusiasm to launch a shot at the men should they try and kill them, but the sky gave nothing, the sky was empty and it was only as I looked back and saw that two of the scarecrows were moving, straining under their binding, fighting against the poles they were attached to, that the awful reality of the situation dawned. I tried to tell myself that if I had known on first sight what was happening, that I would have done something, but I wasn't listening. Talking to myself is one thing but I have never been able to lie to myself for long. I would never have stepped in to stop it and that knowledge, unavoidable as it was, disgusted me every bit as much as my stupidity at looking into the sky for birds. Had I stepped in, I would either have been murderer or victim. Killer or corpse. Is it so wrong to want to be neither? I slumped down against the tree and it sagged away from me, snapping at the base. The gunshots started and the two moving scarecrows began to move faster, a frenzied puppet dance, their rag-tag bodies jerking wildly on the poles, arms falling to the ground, their stuffing spilled outwards, and downwards, and next to them, all the while, their lifeless neighbours stared to the ground, heads bowed, bodies already defeated. As the rifles emptied, the laughter and cheering started, beyond that and above us all, the dying echoes of gunfire penetrated the sky like encroaching thunder.

'The thing I have to have is belief in you and me. We have to believe in each other.'

I should have known from the relieved sigh of my car when I cut the engine on entering the coppice that I

shouldn't have done it and, ready to move out, it took
five minutes of wiggling the keys in the ignition before
I eventually agreed with the obvious and accepted that
the car was dead. She'd played dead before, that was part
of the appeal of the old girl; each frosty morning there
was always a little teasing dance before submission and
I always had the touch, but now I knew things were
different. I gave one last try, a token effort for the cheap
seats, and she coughed and burped and fell back to
silence. The last death judders rumbled out underneath
me and she gave no more. I looked back at the road and
then across it, beyond the cracked tarmac and through
into a field on the other side. It could only be a mile or
so to Butcher's house and cutting across the field might
shave a meaningless amount of time from the ultimately
assumed length to destination. If there were no
scarecrows, it would be worth taking that route. That
was my reasoning. I chose not to let the fact I had no
choice come in to the equation. I gathered up the
rations, kissed the girl on the hood and crossed the road,
entered the field and didn't look back.

The field stretched north and up over a hill and I
began to trudge through oozing mud mounds that were
squeezing the grass out of the picture, my feet
squelching deep and then popping free with every step.
My right shoe had had enough after the tenth step and
I didn't have the energy to try and persuade it back on
to my foot. If I had been thinking straight I probably

would have questioned the wisdom of walking a field fresh from a rain shower, but if I was thinking straight so many things would be different. There were a couple of cow corpses up ahead, perished and skeletal, underneath small black clouds of flies. It often occurs to me how the beast has suffered under the country's destruction – not that they were whooping it up beforehand, of course. Would these poor creatures have preferred to be carved up for the empty fat man's feast? I doubt it. Perhaps there is a dignity in starving to death, free finally from interfering human hands that can't help but build so as to destroy, hollow minds that can't just leave well alone. I felt the plastic smoothness of the sausages from the tin of beans and sausages that I had pathetically wolfed down at Pigeon's house rise slightly from deep below and I felt ashamed.

At the tip of the hill, the field narrowed and a small pathway ran across it past flattened electric fencing and into a deeper patch of woodland. To the other side, the hill dropped steeply then reached a plateau about twenty feet down. On this stretch of field, a few benches were positioned towards a gaping horizon that held the black decaying town I had just left at its swollen lip like a darkening disease. A small pay telescope was rusting between the benches; whatever was to see here was no longer worth paying for.

I remember how Archie used to describe the country. It

seemed nonsensical to me then but has grown more apt with every day. I always knew it was a greedy country, that was obvious, and a selfish one too, of course, but he always used to call it a desperate country. He may have got it right. "I look at it like a ship... A big, big ship," he would say, "a rich man's ship. The country is a ship upended in choppy waters and we are all in the sea, desperately swimming to get back on board and get a grip of the mast, to hold on tight. But there are sharks in the water; as many sharks as there are people. The sharks are hungrier than the people. The sharks want it more. The swimming becomes thrashing. The ship starts to sink. The mast gets smaller..." He would never finish the analogy, perhaps knowing that our own imagination would colour in the spaces better than any words ever could.

I wish I could make it all better for Archie, for us all, I really do, in the past that would have been my job. I was his Mr. Fix-it, his go to man. His bitch. But this... Well, this was just a bit beyond me. He released a plague, did my old mate Archie, when he took away consequence. That was the moment he let us off the lead. He signed us all over to each other to fight it out between ourselves. I told him as much the last time we spoke. He knew, he really did, so don't be unfairly angry towards him. He's a nice fellow when you get to know him. I told him that too. I said, "You know what, Prime Minister, underneath all the meaningless flannel and overwhelming ineptitude, you are actually a decent chap." I hope they can rebuild parliament some time soon. It's iconic. We are going to need things like that, places of that stature when we try and get the tourists back. They like to take photos of places like that. In all honesty, I doubt there will be too much left worth a good damn once the lawyers have finished rifling through the silverware. But we've got to be optimistic, haven't we?

I shouldn't talk about the things that have happened in the country as it always makes me feel like I should draw some sort of conclusion from my ramblings and we all know that such is a foolish endeavour. We are living in the unexplainable, amongst the unaccountable, turning our clocks forward with hesitant hands to a future that no one can quite foresee. We are living off instincts and the most basic of emotions. There is no right or wrong any more and we have handed ourselves over to our worst desires. We are beasts in a temporary freedom. But with that freedom comes an unbearable fragility; you fill your stone cold heart long enough and eventually it will wound and die.

I've just read that back. It sounds pretentious. I'm sorry.

I would like to offer answers to you as you probably think, from my previous lofty position, that I can see better the slit of light on the horizon that will usher all this horror away? I'm afraid you would be disappointed.

I'm nothing any more, just like you. Like everyone. I'm just trying to get by, ploughing my furrow the best way I know how. Trying not to be scared. The pills make it go away for a while but, at time of writing at least, I still have to open my eyes again as I float back down. I'm just trying to survive; aren't you? Just because I'm off the telly I'm not that much better than you. We still have the same goals these days, don't we? We are still the same, more or less.

I had been sat on one of the benches for a few minutes, staring out at the fires raging on the south end of town – the town hall and the shopping arcade if you want details, both now were blackened ribs and nothing much else save a memory – when I noticed an elderly couple sat on the next bench. Some private detective I must be! It was with shock and surprise that I stared at them as the woman made a greeting. If a child were asked to describe an old person, these two were liable to be the outcome, so steeped in pensioner cliché that they were, I half expected to be offered a warm mint. I just stared at them as they stared back, she with a bake-a-cake motherly smile and he with excitable eyes that covered every inch of my muddied, bloodied and bruised body. She spoke again and I was dragged back to reality.

'I said, are you here to watch the fires too? We usually come at this time of the day. He proposed on this bench, didn't you Father?'

'Yes, Mother, this was the bench. Fifty years ago next week.'

'Congratulations,' I said convincingly, without really meaning it.

'We like to come up to this spot and watch the town burn whilst we have our sandwiches. There's not much left anymore; we may have to find another bench soon.'

'I was just saying to Mother, you look familiar, have we met before?'

'I used to be on TV.'

'Oh, the gogglebox, we don't have much time for that, do we, Mother?'

'Certainly not. Nothing but sex and destruction. We prefer a good play.'

'I was also in the last government.' I waved a hand at the horizon, feeling stupid that I had assumed they needed an explanation.

'We don't hold much for politics, do we, Father?'

'We don't. Nothing but sex and destruction. We get enough of that on TV.'

'Well, we don't watch television, though, do we?'

'Oh no, we don't watch it, no. Haven't done in years. Too much sex and destruction.'

'We prefer a good play.'

They seemed so proud of that statement that I let them have it, a small victory for a small couple. It was a big deal to them and, in all honesty, I'm hardly in a position to argue.

'What shows were you on? We used to like the antiques programmes.'

'I did children's shows mainly.'

'Oh I see, how lovely.'

'At the start, then I moved on to mainstream shows.'

'Anything we might have seen?'

'I presented "Celebrity Abortion", that was quite popular.'

'Oh dear, oh dear, oh dear.'

'And "Nutcase", do you remember that? We would put a celebrity in a locked room with a gun and see how long..."

'Oh dear me, no. I don't think we know those shows.'

'Do I disgust you?'

'No, dear. Why ever would you think that?'

'I disgust myself. I just wondered how I was wearing it.'

'Would you care for a sandwich?'

We sat and ate sandwiches and watched the town blacken and blend into the early evening gloom. A rain cloud was forming and light rain came like frustrated tears from up above. Mother and Father put on their coats and huddled close, staring out at the horizon like they were sat in an art gallery soaking up an old master's masterpiece rather than a new fool's mistake. I watched them cuddling in and felt jealous. I had often pictured how Albie and I would look in old age; had wondered where we would go and what we would do. I had looked forward to those intimate cuddles, those moments of complete togetherness, bound by age and the knowing that even if there was something better out there we were too old to be bothered to find it.

I finished my sandwich and was set to head off, thank them and forget them when Mother started tapping the bench between her and Father. 'Sit, my dear, sit with us.'

'Indeed, young man, you must sit. We can watch the view together.'

Despite initial reluctance and a healthy dose of suspicion from my default setting, I took the bench between them and let Mother wrap me in a warm embrace that instantly made me feel light headed. She started to stroke my hair as I leant against her chest and snuggled in. Father tapped my knee in a manly fashion and leant back on the bench kicking his legs out to full stretch. We watched the old cinema in the town explode into an angry amber fireball and slowly dismantle under the lead coloured mushroom of smoke that punched out into the wet tar sky. Thunder rolled, lighting struck and the rain gradually changed from a tickle to a thump.

'I do still love you. I really do. When I was young that used to be enough for anyone.'

I slept against her comforting chest. As the rain drew in

heavy, she raised an umbrella to shield me. I was back at the blue house instantly, almost as if sleep was the corner in a dark corridor that I had to turn. The comfort of familiar had always been there at that house, but now it was intense. I seemed to be running two dreams in parallel as another scene began to be superimposed over the top. Voices were muddled and confusing, images at my eyes out of focus. In one instance I was standing outside the house, staring up at the flickering light, and the next I was sat there, in that room, opposite Archie, a weak candlelight fluttering away between us. We both looked old, really old, beaten and shrunk. We spoke as friends even though the set-up was more befitting an interview; our two chairs positioned opposite each other and a small crate upturned in the middle with a candle on top. The room was a defeated room, cracked and stripped of all that mattered. Our chairs sat on a shaky floor and at any moment it felt the room could tip over. Our conversation was an old conversation; there were words I knew, feelings I remembered.

'I'm sorry, Zach, really I am.'

'Have we broken a country?'

'I said I'm sorry.'

'It's not a password.'

'It's all I have. I made a mistake and there is no going back.'

'A mistake? Is that supposed to make it better? At least convince me you did it with great meaning, like it were the last and only original idea left in the world.'

The flame between us puffed out as if a door had been opened and a breeze ushered in. I looked for a door, felt for a breeze, then looked to my left at the missing wall, spilling down to the garden below, and knew that I was mistaken. About much, no doubt, and certainly this. The candlelight came back on like a child's joke candle at a birthday party.

'Are you well, Zach? Still taking the pills?'

'You mean, am I officially mad yet?'

'How is Albie?'

'I believe she's fine. I don't know. How's Albie, Prime Minister?'

'Call me Archie.'

'Albie.'

'You shouldn't be here. It's not safe.'

'Nowhere is, not now.'

'No.'

'We are still here though, aren't we?'

'We are.'

'Maybe that's how you get free of it. Maybe that's how you survive?'

'How?'

'Be the last man standing.'

'I'm sorry, Zachary. If I had anything about me, I would ask you to shoot me.'

'I don't work for you anymore, boss.'

'Don't call me that. That indicates complicity.'

'Sorry, Archie.'

'And that indicates friendship.'

'But you were my friend.'

'Surely a luxury in these crazy days.'

The candlelight went out again and did not come back on. I felt across the crate for Archie but could feel nothing. Outside the shattered wall, the sky was a dreamy soft black, dotted with stars. The moon was full and bright but gave nothing to the room. I stood and felt the floor begin to tip. I tried to sit again but missed the chair and landed on my side. I called out to Archie, to Albie, to anyone. Shouted and screamed.

'How do I get out of here?' I yelled to the floor. 'Someone give me an answer, someone tell me what to do!'

With that I was awake, jumping up instantly and hitting my head on the bench, which, in the absence of Mother and Father, was now my shield from the rain. From the world.

'Hello? Are you there?'

By the time I left the bench and headed across the north end of the field, night had come on and gone out and the grey, dreary dawn that has become the norm was all around; the relentless darkness of night had been sucked away, trapped until an hour that was yet to invite it back. Mother and Father had left a small cake for me that I greedily crammed down on waking, instantly regretting the selfish speed and wishing I could thank them. It was chocolate and as light as the air used to be. With so many broken streetlights it was hard, in the congealing drabness, to see where I was going. I held Pigeon's bottle of Scotch in one hand and could hear it sloshing loudly as I walked. I knew on waking that I had drunk some of it. I couldn't remember it, but I could feel it at the back of my throat. The gentle burning that once gave comfort now felt like acid, its pungent fumes pouring in to my empty head like smoke in a sealed glass jar.

I stumbled out of the field on to a country lane, a row of half-standing houses were in the distance and I knew that, if memory served, Butcher's home would be one of them. I also knew that my memory was not what it once was and served only itself. I could be miles away from anything or just around the corner. I necked back another glug of Scotch and found the confidence not to care either way. I walked on, slapping my shoeless right foot into puddles on the uneven road, desperately gripping the bottle of Scotch like a drowning man would grip debris.

The village was dead, the houses deceased, the heart hollow. I walked past an old bandstand and saw a tuba sat alone. The quick glimpse, for that was all I allowed, brought the tears back and I didn't try to fight them anymore. Children's bikes lay scattered across an old green; there was a small push-tractor upended in someone's front garden, and a gnome, a dear old gnome, casting his fishing line onto cracked concrete in someone else's drive. Half his head was sheared off and he had a ridiculous grin on his face. It was this sight that reminded me of the rubber duck and I pulled it from my coat pocket and held it close. I could feel eyes on me, I knew I wasn't alone, I knew that something was here; if I had confidence in myself I would have said I could hear voices, but with me that could just mean I was thinking.

A low-level mist hung across all and I could feel it trying to wash my bones as I pushed on slowly, convincing myself that I knew where I was going and that what I was doing was obvious. I took another swig of Scotch and let the fake self-confidence nibble back the self-disgust. The damaged houses leered at me through the mist; size confused in the spooky half-light and each and every one became a house of horrors in a deserted funfair that was neither fun nor fair. I strained to listen to the dawn chorus but could pick up nothing. There is no more ominous and terrifying a sound than the sound of no birdsong in the morning. You get used to the gunfire and the screaming, but I have yet to meet the man that could smile in this silence.

I reached the end of the road and stumbled against a postbox. A small carpet of post was at my feet and more threatened to tumble out of the stuffed postbox mouth. I wondered how many letters of love lay there unread, how many promises and pleas, how many people are now walking a different route for one small sentence they never read, or one small communication from a loved one they weren't aware of. As much as such could break a heavy heart, I found myself smiling at the very basic idea that people were still writing letters to each other. There was still hope; it was just well hidden.

I was looking at it before I realised I had seen it a hundred times before. The dirty blue paint of the front, the missing wall, spilling out into the garden. Butcher's house was in front of me. I looked up through the exposed rooms, trying to find the flickering light, trying to complete the dream that had stalked me for so long, but there was no light. There was merely a suffocating darkness. I knew, even before I told myself, that I was too late. I looked further up and saw that the roof was bent in on itself as if punched through by a giant, the windows blown inwards, like eyes burnt out of a corpse. I stepped back into the shadows for a moment and watched the road. The voices seemed to have gone but I couldn't shift the feeling of being watched. Paranoia in my job is healthy, of course; it sharpens the edges and keeps you on your feet. The problem is that, with the way my legs are, that isn't always ideal. I waited a good five minutes, ten minutes in all, before clambering into Butcher's front garden, stumbling across the crazy brick tongue that was sticking mockingly out of the front door, and letting the house swallow me up.

I crossed a long hall that spread out underneath higgledy-piggledy stairs. I was aware of talking from somewhere and quickly ducked back into the shadows again, straining my eyes and somehow hoping to hear better. It was a woman's voice, low and tinny, as if sealed in a prison. It was a good couple of minutes before I realised it was my Dictaphone.

'I need you to want me again. If you wanted me, you could find me.'

I wandered through all the rooms downstairs and, apart from the odd chair, odd in its normality, there was nothing, not even a television. The kitchen had fallen into the lounge, the cheap units standing on their sides against the back wall. The sink was sat on the sofa. A hole in the lounge wall looked in to the neighbouring house. The floorboards bore glass and splinters. Pools of water gathered in the uneven surfaces. I took to the stairs.

'We all make mistakes, you and I more than most. If we had to stall at each mistake, we would still be in youth. Can you not forgive? I know you can forget. I did.'

On the landing, I felt myself tilting slightly as the walls seemed to close in. The attic door was open but the holes in the ceiling showed nothing worth investigating. In the spare room there was nothing; in the bathroom not even a bath, and I turned to the last room on the landing and drew my pistol. As I neared, a circular shadow was visible on the carpet and then there was that smell again, the smell that lingers at the edge of everything nowadays, a poison pumped in to the air by us all. It was the smell of death and it was hanging around the edges of that room. I stood on a floorboard that creaked and I made myself jump and drop the gun, as I bent down timidly to pick it up I could see the shadow was not a shadow but a circle of dried blood, and from the level of the floor a pair of feet could be seen next to it. I drew to my full height, which was never going to be tall enough, not here, held the pistol in front of me at the end of an extended but shaking arm, stepped forward, stepped quietly, and stepped in.

The body, a man's body, dressed in a revolting off-yellow shirt and beige slacks, was face down on the carpet, a single gunshot to the back of his neck. His arms spread forward, reaching for a large kitchen knife just out of reach. As I crossed into the room, my eyes were drawn to a cheap ornament on a shelf above the bed, something so worthless that even the looters didn't want it: a golden plastic wrench mounted on a cheap base. I looked down at Butcher and then at the pistol in my hand, the hammer cocked back against the one empty chamber. I had been here before, I had dreamt this time and again, but now when I needed reality I couldn't wake up. I circled the room almost as if I expected to find her hiding in one of the corners, ready to jump out of the shadows. I searched the air in vain for a trace of perfume, something that indicated she had ever been here, but the corpse at my feet was all that there was to see or smell. I ran back out on to the landing and searched the rooms again before returning to the bedroom and falling to my knees at Butcher's prone body, bent comical and shaded grotesque, the stiffness of his body seemed as fragile as the floorboards breaking underneath us. I hit him twice on the back and screamed at him. "Where is she?" I repeated again and again into the back of his head. "Tell me where she is, you fucking bastard!" Does it count if you swear at a corpse? Don't judge me. Or if you do, then please remember where I came from, okay? On and on I went, crying myself hoarse and spluttering out my desperation over tears that never seemed to be ending. My legs gave and spread out limp under my backside. I fell back and hit the floor hard, the hand still holding the gun falling against my knee with a force I couldn't feel. I cried until it was painful, I wept snot to my chin, as my head cleared, memories and emotions pouring from my ears until I was a shell, ready to be corrupted or stamped on.

Hours passed as I lay next to Butcher breathing in the worst smell there could ever be. The day came quietly and faded out with just as little fanfare. The Dictaphone played itself flat on my chest, the words close enough to hurt but just far enough away to trick into a dream. She was all I could think about. All that mattered. I needed to see her, I needed to find her. Somehow there would be answers in that. She could tell me that all was well. I pulled myself up, moving gently against the wall and stared out into the night, out into a village that had long since given up and towards a horizon that seemed to pulse with the last heartbeats of life. She was out there somewhere. I had to find her. Her voice gnawed away at me, the hurt was a hollowness that needed to be filled. The floor began to break under me and I stepped back in a hurry as a floorboard snapped, tilted up and gently slipped down the rubble trail to the garden below. I reasoned it would be about a day's worth of walking to get back home. Perhaps I would get lucky and someone would offer me a lift. At that thought, I remembered Edgerton and the envelope he had given me. I took it from my jacket and stared at the sealed mouth; it was no longer smiling. He had said it would change the world, perhaps it would, and perhaps he was mad. Perhaps that was the answer. It's usually madmen that change the world. But I was sane, what right did I even have to try?

'Where are you, Zach? I hope you are safe. I hope you are well. I hope you are alive.'

I got back to Apple Avenue within the next day and cleaned my cuts and bruises at the kitchen sink. I had to set off again and meet my next punter and I always try and look presentable, even nowadays. He had said he needed to find his wife and I had said I was more than happy to try. I couldn't find my watch and had no way of knowing whether I was going to be late or early. In that freedom of ignorance I decided to grab five minutes in my armchair, nestling into the arse print like it were a gloved hand and resting my eyes, letting the last of the pills kick around my soul. I would have to get some more from somewhere and perhaps if this job allowed I would find the time. I do love my job. I'm good at my job. The best. There is nothing like reuniting love to make you feel worthwhile. The jobs aren't so plentiful these days, certainly not the jobs that bring love back together. If I wanted to be a conduit to murder I could probably be a millionaire by now. That's all people want. Everyone is either a killer or a corpse and I'm trying my damndest to be different. Stupid me. But still, while the work is there I'm going to try and enjoy it. I need to promote myself, I need to advertise, people would hire me if they knew about me. I used to be on the TV and people buy anything if your face fits. People don't phone anymore, but I'm confident that they would if they could. People don't write letters either and that's a very sad thing, isn't it? People don't communicate. People don't care. But I'm going to make a go of this business. I'm going to buy a nice big house and a swimming pool like Albie always wanted. I'm going to make her proud of me.

I put the envelope amongst my papers. I would get around to it but it would have to wait. The job has to come first. The job always has to come first. I'm not fit to change the world, anyway. I'm nobody. Right now it's all about surviving and for me it's the job that does that. The rest of the country will have to find its own way. I will leave that up to more intelligent people to figure out. Albie would probably know what to do. If I knew where she was, I'd ask her. I miss her. I miss her love and I miss her friendship. She'd know how to survive this. She would have a better solution than my contribution to the cause when the walls started to fall, "you escape this by being the last man standing," that's what I told Archie. What a fool I was. Obviously the last man standing will be a lawyer. We will have to find another way.

Albie's Verse

In the beginning...

It was the word, then the word had to be put in writing, the writing put in triplicate and the whole damn lot sent care of the law firm of Schuttler and Wise, a team of criminally bland men in an obscenely large office, deciding our country's future with contemplative chin strokes and rabid self interest. I suppose, looking at it that way, it was just politics in better ties. We had gone from a nanny state to a babysitter state without anyone having time to blink. Poor old Archie. It wasn't totally his fault, I think it really was the lawyers – well, the lawyers and his ineptitude. Or perhaps it was our starry-eyed fickle foolishness. I suppose I don't really know. I prefer blaming the lawyers. I'd feel sorry for Archie if he was someone else.

My dad always wanted me to marry a lawyer. Or a Jew, or a Scot – someone who knew the value of money, he said. My father did like a good stereotype and cliché. He was a bigot. He'd have been horrified to know I ended up with a children's TV presenter; to him, children's TV presenters were either gay or borderline serial killers. He lived in broad strokes, my father. He died of a stroke. No one found it ironic. "Money doesn't make the world go round, Alberta," he would say, "but it should be respected, just as you would respect a ravenous tiger if you were sitting on its head with your pants off. A man that sees life in those terms should be held on to. Make him happy, Alberta. Keep away from bankers." I did date a banker once; a virgin of twenty years' standing with an Oedipal fixation. He would holiday with his mother and in all honesty it was all a little seedy. She had a face like a threadbare quilt; he a penis like the beak of a Puffin. I only saw it once but once was enough. My dad was right about them, or right about him at least, as he had no idea about money. He spent and spent and spent – jumpers, mostly. Occasionally he bought shoes, brown shoes, always brown shoes. I'm not sure what that says about a man.

By the time I met Zach, they had more or less written me off as a lesbian. I never bothered to explain why I wasn't bringing guys home for them to run the rule over; it was just easier to keep quiet and let them think I was a Maybe Mavis. My dad would have assumed I was Zach's cover; my mum that he was the last throw of the dice for a desperate girl. Zach wasn't much to look at back then; he had a rugged charm, at the start at least, but then he became a whore to himself and self-image started making him ugly. But I clung on in there and I fought the good fight. At least I thought, at the time, there was something worth fighting for, and that is always half the battle. Poor old Zach, "the thinking man's second thought", that's what they ended up calling him. If anyone had told us back then, back when we were doing kids' TV, when he was wearing floral shirts and I had my hand up a puppet's arsehole, that we would have become TV's golden couple, I'd have thought you were nuts.

I don't feel guilty about what I did, which is the thing I feel most guilty about. But I wish I had ended it sooner; it would have been better all round. Ten years should count for something. Even just counting to ten. I talk to my friends about it and they just tell me to cling to the good times and let the rest go. My friends, the ones in long relationships, that is – and there are disconcertingly few – all tell me they bookmark their lives through their relationships, you know, things they did, places they went, emotions they felt; they are all little post-it notes on their lives. Then there's me and Zach, every move, every comment, every emotion plastered in the press, displayed on the TV like last week's prize turkey, everything we did recorded and stored, edited, rearranged and moulded into something interesting and something I can't recall. I look back at us then from this false position now and it looks like a story played out by badly fitting actors. My Albie doesn't even have particularly white teeth. That is not to say I wasn't happy, because I expect I might have been in phases. He was a good guy, Zach; he was always a little left of centre but it's only recently that he's been taking the lunacy to town. But where's the blame? He's in good company, as so many of us have. Well, you know all this, of course; it's been all over the TV these last few months. The country fell apart and we all just watched. The TV was there every step of the way, waiting for us to jump on board, ready to watch us crack. I won't crack, though. No way. I want no part of this any more. When they open the ports and the airports again then I'm out of here. Anywhere that will have me.

When they tried to get us out of the capital – that's those of us that were deemed worthy of saving, and that I was amongst that crowd gives more guilt than I know what to do with – they tried to take us north on two private trains. There were about two hundred of us in total, strangers by and large, united in nothing but their worthiness and their fear. We got about thirty miles before the trains came under attack. That we even got that far was a miracle.

I was sat next to Archie's PA Estelle. Indeed it was dear Estelle that got me on board the train in the first place; it was her that used her clout to put my name forward and such kindness, such generosity, meant so much to me that I automatically felt worthless. Estelle was a good person, though it can't have been being good that made you worthy, that certainly was not the criteria – if it was then the trains would have been deserted.

I'd packed just one small bag but Estelle had found it harder to decide what was necessary and had come with a trunk and two sports bags. Some harassed guard had blocked her at the doors and wrestled the trunk from her, spilling the contents across the platform and shoving Estelle in to me and on to the train. She tried to fight back but within seconds there was a crowd behind us trying to push past to the best seats and another, larger crowd, on the platform rooting through her scattered belongings. She cried for the first five miles. I find it strange the importance that some people place on belongings these days. People think nothing of trampling over dead bodies or turning their backs to people's pleas, yet would cut the fingers off anyone who tried to rifle so much as a teabag from their kitchen. We are catering for the self now and we are creating monsters. Maybe we were always that way. We have always been good at suppressing filth with a smile and fury with a token good deed. People have spent so long trying to secure their own place in heaven that they have neglected to consider what they would do if they had to go through hell first.

For a long time, I said nothing to Estelle. I let the view from the train window have my full attention; the shadowed people on the platform, the crazy hopelessness in their faces, the buildings aflame on the horizon, many miles behind them but creeping closer. All these things made my heart beat faster, but none more than the children on the platform, running up and down without a care in the world, disinterested in their parents' concerns, unaware of their encroaching responsibilities, playing at being children as the murky day closed around them. The sky that seemed so close to us looked like ink poured into clear water, the clouds slowly building and blooming, suffocating all that was clean. At random intervals, a small explosion would bleach spots in the clouds and, underneath the clouds, lightning seemed to be looking for a way through. It was the sky of Armageddon as described by TV–trained minds, yet the end that was playing out beneath it was nothing so dramatic; it was the most basic of horror and the sky was either a reflection or a coincidence.

I do like a sunset. They say tomorrow is going to be sunny. Sunshine for days I shouldn't wonder, so maybe it will put people in a better frame of mind. Maybe this will all blow over, because it's got to really – hasn't it? Unless it's all a lie. Perhaps it won't be sunny after all. The weatherman can lie as easily as the next man. You learn the lie in your formative years in the TV industry; you learn to say it, to decipher it, and finally you learn to turn it to a truth. It can be tough schooling and many don't get it as most aren't built for that life and they let it destroy them. I took to TV with ease. I've lied so much to so many people over the years, sometimes intentional, sometimes through habit, that the truth sometimes sounds like a joke missing a punchline. Though I suppose it's a bit like a stopped clock, isn't it?

Occasionally it must have been right. I still think of myself as a child of television, despite all and everything that has gone on, as I was so young when I started that I can't really remember much else, and I haven't actually done anything else. That's something I try not to think about too much. Self-disgust is no friend to progress, and we must all progress – when we finally work out where to go.

That I would go from there to here is vaguely ridiculous, I know that, but that's what TV does, isn't it? It changes lives, it creates people, it shapes and defines, and if you're not savvy enough it can corrupt and destroy as well. I knew the game because I'd done my homework, and I knew what I was doing and where I was going; it's tricky but you can still navigate a course even in shallow waters. It was premeditated at the start. I had my five-year plan and wonderful legs, I climbed high and trod on many, I was good at my job. Even back at the start I had more professionalism and dedication to my craft than most. People have no idea how hard it is being a personality these days. There is no training for that. The TV personality is a much undervalued occupation.

I knew I had the edge on Zach when we first met, but I saw a good man before I ever saw a lovelorn fool. We first got it together one night at the TV studio. It was a forgettable fumble, dirty and quick; so quick in fact that I hadn't even taken Mr. Chuff off my hand. He never said as much but I think for him it added a little something. Then before I knew it we were a double act of sorts. One went with the other and the limited imagination of TV executives couldn't see past it. We were one all-consuming entity of entertainment! We became the latest fashion accessory. How the heck did that happen? Cameras outside the house, stories in the paper and our privacy raped. It was a whirlwind that neither of us really had a handle on; it just rolled and rolled and gathered us up and took us along. Money will do that and fame will do that. People giving you things for free, telling you that you are wonderful will do that. Vanity is a drug only slightly less addictive than the drug of a free ride and I think that became the ultimate ambition for everyone; wealth without work, fame without talent, reward from the willingness to trade out all that makes you whole. I'm a hypocrite, I suppose. Celebrities shouldn't have morals. I'm a poster girl for prostitution without penetration. I never went that far, at least. I never needed to.

When I was a girl, celebrity seemed unobtainable, as it should. You had to have an edge, you had to have a professional work ethic and you had to put the hours in. Nowadays, of course, all that has changed and that I may have played a part in that free-for-all circus revolts me. I feel ashamed that I was too busy feeding the legend to see what I was involved in. No, that's not true; I saw it, I was all too aware of it, what disgusts me is that

I was too scared of my reality to try and stop it. It was my goddaughter that changed things for me, but by then it was too late. When I saw what my goddaughter was becoming, I was already several years, and a hundred bad decisions past the moral high ground.

My goddaughter idolised me and thinking of it now it makes my skin crawl. I corrupted her, I led her down a street paved with fool's gold and she loved it. I tried to train her, I tried to put her on the right path, but she just wouldn't listen. She just saw the lights, the glossies, the adoration and the money. I just saw myself. She told her careers teacher at fourteen that she "wanted to be famous", and he asked her as what? She said it didn't matter. She could have found a cure for cancer, but, well, it was easier to do reality TV I suppose; pump in the plastic, pop the fun bags out in some low-end rhythm rag and then become the biggest bane to the footballer's life since the three-syllable word. That got her in the door and I kept it wedged open. But then the vultures began to circle around her. Naivety is a bell round the neck of prey. She traded her innocence to a casting director of thirty eight for two lines in a period drama based on a book I hadn't read and she hadn't heard of written by a man who was actually a woman. She had no interest for it and not much talent for it either, if I'm being harsh, but she was a hurricane, my little goddaughter; a ferocious force of nature and she kicked up dust wherever she went. It was just the choices she made. There was no quality control and she took everything and everyone that came her way. Grist to the mill, I suppose. The footballers, the boy band singers and the soap stars – they were just the public wreckage of a young girl who didn't know what she was doing. But I look at her now and it breaks my heart, because for better or worse I had created her. She traded on our relationship, articulating the tenuous connection to established fame, which of course you must do if you are to survive in the business, and don't already have the get-out-of-jail-free card of a famous surname. I let her, of course I did. What was I to do? After all, I had been little better; perhaps just as wild but merely in a more conservative time. Back then, of course, there were also other stories in the newspapers so I had to work just that little bit harder.

"I'm okay, Aunt Albie! I know what I'm doing!" Her best acting role was that of an adult, and even in that you could see the joins. Maybe it's just my guilt that makes me weep for her, or maybe it's the memories of that untarnished little girl I watched growing up. I think of her mother, my friend; I think of her father, that humble man. I think of them hiding their shame in false shows of pride. I think I couldn't do it. I think I would tell her. That beautiful girl, damaged by the need to attract attention, the need to still be viable. Her beauty ruined by plastic fakery and impatience, an unwillingness to let the imagination take the strain. But

I could never tell her she had been ruined. I couldn't tell her she looks an abomination. I couldn't. But she does. She's a freak show and everyone's watching.

Estelle cried herself to sleep, slouched in the seat, her sports bag under her head. I gazed around the carriage at the other worthy people; wanting to ask them so much why they were here, what it was that some officious individual, lacking individuality but owning a nice suit, saw in them to put them on this train. Across from Estelle and I, a young couple spoke in low whispers, their hands clasped together they pulled each other close, their eyes nowhere but on the other's face; nowhere in the world more important to be, nothing more vital to see. In front of them, two young men were busy at their mobiles, each tapping away in finger frenzy, every once in a while turning to the other and showing them their phone. No one seemed to be speaking. Despite the odd murmur, the carriage gave nothing. It made me want to stand up and shout, but I had nothing to say. Outside the window, the dark countryside blurred past, fleeting stretches of blackness, brushing past the pale reflection of my face without giving detail. I suddenly needed to move, needed to get out of my seat. The carriage seemed to be closing in on me, the recycled air churning in slow laboured rhythms, the dull murmuring from my neighbours a persistent buzzing at my ears. I began to rub the sweat from my hands onto my trousers, my fingers were twitching, eyes pricking, feet ballooning in my shoes, and there was a scream close to my lips. I half stood and stumbled over Estelle's sleeping body, clambering into the aisle. My foot caught in Estelle's other sports bag and I tripped forward, barging my shoulder in to the conspiratorial lovers. The lights in the carriage stuttered, went out and then clicked back. I bowed my head, wrapped my arms around my body and strode out of the carriage with as much speed and dignity as I could manage.

The next carriage was silent; every head was either turned to the window or to their lap, and there was no sound beyond the steady engine of the train and the occasional whisper. People were on phones and laptops, their faces set in concentration; some rested their heads on the tables between the seats and pretended to sleep. Luggage was clogging the aisle and the luggage racks were stacked high and clumsy. I weaved my way through, over legs and around cases and bags, steadying myself on the backs of seats and trying desperately not to trip over again. I must have looked drunk to anyone who was watching. Someone must have been. There is always someone watching.

Beyond was the buffet car. It was empty but for a small man in a clip-on bow tie who clearly wanted to be elsewhere. He was wrapping clingfilm over plastic plates of food and trying to stop a long tower of cups from teetering over. I let the air of the empty carriage flood over me for a second before resting myself against the wall and breathing in deeply. The small man was watching me. I could feel him from the corner of my eyes; he either wanted to register recognition or offer food. Either way, I wanted him to go away. The train jolted and I stumbled backwards. Hands were instantly at my hips, steadying me; I could feel my body tighten against them, the rage well up, the fists clench. I made to turn to the small man and swing a punch at him, but as I turned, it was another man I was looking at – a freak, my father would have said. My father was a wise man.

'Are you okay, Albie?'

He was batty-eyed and unkempt, the sort of human blancmange who would argue about politics and yet run away screaming from a hedge. He quickly retracted his hands from my hips and stuffed them into his pockets. I struggled to place the face, so let him do the talking. He seemed good at it.

'My name's Edgerton. I've been trying to find you. You have no idea how hard it was to secure a passage on this train. I have to give you something.'

'You really don't.'

'I do.'

'Do you know who I am?'

'Yes, that's how I know I have to give you something. I tried to give it to Archie, but circumstance separated us. I need this to be given to someone with power.'

'I have no power.'

'But you're a celebrity. You have more power than anyone.'

'Did Archie put you up to this?'

'Archie? No. Dear me, no. Archie is a dear friend, a good man.'

'Well, let's not stretch that truth too far, Edgerton.'

'We were together but we got…'

'Separated, you said, and I was uninterested the first time. Please go away.'

'I know you and he were close.'

'He was my boss.'

'Yes, that as well.'

'I wouldn't believe all you may have heard or read.'

'Would that we all ignored the mass media Albie, if we did would we be here right now, running away in fear?'

'What do you want?'

'I don't blame you for all that's happened.'

'How kind. I know you, don't I?'

'We have met.'

'How do you know Archie? Did you work for him too?'

'I used to. Now I work for the man, the main man.'

'The man?'

'He gave me something. I must give it to you. We must change the world and you can be the one to do it.'

'No thanks. Been there, done that.'

'And made a mess of it. This is your chance for redemption. Only the mad would not want the chance to make things better, to cleanse their soul. Only the very maddest madman.'

'And you are the face of sanity?'

The lights in the carriage went out before he could answer. At first I thought it nothing but a welcome excuse to avoid Edgerton, I imagined slipping away from him in the darkness, hiding away back amongst the silent people and hoping he would latch his madness on to another. But relief was only temporary. I tried to turn and walk away but all of a sudden my feet were off the ground and I felt like I was floating. The air squeezed in to my face and I was tilting forward, my head and shoulder blade colliding with the wall, and then I was turning in the air, spinning at speed, the darkness folding around me and the false air sucking me into empty space like a pebble tossed into a well. There was an unearthly thud as something broadsided the train, those silent and worthy hundreds now alive and screaming as one. The realisation didn't come to me until some hours later, but we had now reached a time where there was no longer any comfort to be derived from being deemed worthy. That was quite a milestone for England to achieve and it seemed to slip into being without anyone noticing. If you escape, if you survive, if you persevere, it is luck, not status; it is good fortune and not personal fortune. We are all in it together. It took the country to break for us all to be the most united we had ever been.

I try and be optimistic. This is just a little anarchy. They will blow themselves out eventually, of course they will; they have to because this can't be sustained, this is just a fad, it has to level out and we have to tilt upright again. None of this is my fault, of course; it's important to know that. I was there but the blame must be another's. Fuck, I sound like a politician. I'm not. I'm not anyone, not any more; I'm no one and I don't count. It wasn't my idea and I didn't create all this, you don't shoot the messenger... And I was a damn good presenter! I was a personality! I showed Zach. I showed them all that I could do it alone! Men! Always men! Oh, I heard the whispering, I'm not stupid. "Zach made you, darling," they'd all say to me. "You'd never have got anywhere without the man by your side." It's a particularly female affliction, you see? It never works the other way around. There is still a 1950's sensibility you've got to turn off before you get to these enlightened times. I tried so hard not to be a cliché, to not be one of those dreadful women whose very existence is defined by a man, the whiny, moany, lazy plot devices in a male love letter. It's not a man's world; don't ever let people con you into that fallacy. Men just shout louder. My father told me that. Men! Everywhere and always at every corner; girlfriend, daughter, stooge and whore. "He who shouts loudest has the least to say," my father said once, "and he who listens has the least to offer." I'm not entirely sure what he meant. He may have got that from a cracker. He was a dinner party sage, my father. If the country had let him fight wars from his armchair, so many lives would have been saved.

My father could have been a great man if he had had the breaks of a better schooling, had he not married at eighteen and had he not allowed his life to be corrupted by a speedboat. All things considered, it's a slightly more exciting destruction than that which we are facing now; although it came from greed, it came from self-interest and grotty base instincts, so maybe there isn't that much of a difference. Who wants a fucking speedboat, anyway? Fat old sugar daddies in linen suits with a knuckle pecker between their legs and a high maintenance tart hanging off their arm, that's your speedboat crowd. Not a middle-aged dustman, well, a refuse collector, an environmental enforcer – whatever the lawyer speak is nowadays. Bastard lawyers; I bet they have speedboats. That speedboat was what started me in showbiz, you know? Course you do, you probably read about it in one of my autobiographies. It's still hilarious to think I had a five-book publishing deal! Me? That's more than I've read! Still, it's only books, it's only words. None of it matters.

It was my father's drinking buddy Les that wanted to go on the quiz show where they ended up winning the speedboat. My father didn't, never a man to push himself forward, my father. He only went on in the end for me. I must have been such a vulgar little foot-stomping, hair-pulling bitch when I was a kid. I choose not to remember. He did most things I asked of him. Maybe he wanted a quiet life, maybe he loved me, and maybe I was just a monster. I don't know. But I wanted to go to a TV studio so I told him to go on the show and he did as he was told. If they hadn't succeeded, had they come a glorious second, maybe won some money, a bit of change and tat, things would have been so different. But they won the big daddy of the prizes and that was what started it all. They won! That day they were the best. We had never been the best at anything. I still feel guilty now about how that speedboat broke their friendship, I really do. Whatever way you want to cut that cake, it's my fault they didn't speak for years. We never wanted a speedboat. Dad couldn't even swim. Mum doesn't like the water, she says it just makes her want to piss, but none of that mattered, of course, once they had won it. Logic became irrelevant.

That speedboat changed him, changed us, and he wouldn't let it go. Les wanted it, Dad wanted it, Mum and Mrs. Les just wanted them to sell it and split the cash. But that speedboat represented something more than money. It was a symbol of wealth more powerful than anything they had known. It was being wealthy enough to own something you had no use for and they fought in the streets, they shouted over fences and then, as if sent from hell's darkest corner, came the merry men of the law to referee and go through our dirty laundry and pick over the bones of our dignity. In the end, Mum firebombed the boat one night, but Dad had already got the materialistic hard-on and there was no going back. It started as one-upmanship with Les; it was having a nicer car, bigger TV, better clothes, but that game only stretched as far as his paypacket, and he soon needed an easier route and a different angle. He needed a no-holds-barred, no-education-needed, talent-free wealth bonanza. He needed TV. "But I'm an old twazok, I don't fit on TV. They won't want me. It's all about glamour nowadays. It's all about tight tops and loose morals. We need another angle. Albie, dear? I think we should get your teeth whitened." That was my first introduction to the world of television. Over five years I won them hampers, seven sets of steak knives, two caravans, four holidays and a set of golf clubs. But no speedboats. It was while I was on the last of those quiz shows that I met Zach in the TV show canteen. I was working for him two weeks later.

I'm glad my father can't see what's become of us, that I'd been a part of it, no matter how small; he'd be so disappointed in me and that in itself would be worse than all the rioting, the murder and the lies. That my part was small in the whole affair would have made little difference to him, "There are no small parts in grand events, Alberta. Every small cog plays a part in turning the machine." He was a wise man, my father; perhaps if he had been Prime Minister instead we might have swerved this little problem. Or perhaps if someone with integrity had done the job it might have been different, perhaps anyone at all – anyone but Archie. They say each generation gets the leaders it deserves, so perhaps Archie, or some variation, was always going to pick up the reins. We got what we created.

I was lying on my back in a field when my senses came back to earth. The damp grass was soaking my clothes, my hair was wet and matted and my bones were wailing at me. Above, the sky was thick; close enough to let your hand dance through it, it seemed, and I wanted to reach up and comb the blackness out of it, to blow away the clouds, to scratch my nails across it and let some light in. I tried to stand but slipped over on the slick grass and tumbled onto my side. There were bodies in front of me, large mounds of shapes just beyond them. Further on, a figure in flames was charging up and down a large bank, intermittently rolling in the grass, trying to subdue the angry amber. Figures were moving in the darkness, quick and agile; people were fighting other people, clumsily thumping and kicking. Small cracking noises hit the air and every now and again someone would shout, but no words made sense. Nothing made sense. I turned to my front and buried my hands in the earth, closing my fingers in the soil to find purchase, yanking my body forward inch by inch. I wedged my heels into the ground to provide force behind me, and small piles of earth, ploughed by my chin, built up at my mouth. It was the moment I would always look back on to remind me how far I had fallen; the sensation I always went back to whenever I felt that I wanted to step back into the world again. I knew from that moment on that I just wanted to hide.

Behind me, two carriages were on their sides, teetering at the tip of a large wet bank, the lights inside flickering with a pathetic timidity. Shadows moved amongst them, long warped shapes being thrown at the windows. I thought of Estelle, my dear friend, and a coldness drained down me at the thought of where she might be now. I shoved myself on, trying not to think of anything that might stop me and make me concede, but it was hopeless. My energy had gone; there was no strength any more, my body was shrieking its confusion and refusing to comply. I stopped and rolled onto my back, waiting for the soft earth to collapse inwards and gobble me up.

As I lay there, I began counting to myself. I don't know why, perhaps it doesn't matter why, but some part of me seemed to want to mark the length of time I was there, as if it would somehow mean something to someone someday. It was foolish, but it was a distraction of the mind so served that purpose, if not anything logical. Time has begun to mean less and less these days. I had assumed it was still daytime, but the sky was saying different. I counted to ten minutes, more or less, before I fell asleep. I have no idea, no way of giving an informed guess as to how long I lay in that field. When I woke, my clothes were drenched and hugged me like an extra skin; my hair was over my face, curled ends in my mouth like a pipe. I could taste the horrid steely flavour of blood and my bones felt as if they had snapped to a million pieces and been glued back in the wrong places. I had been moved and was now lying in a country lane, my arms crossed over my chest as if I had expired and was ready to be viewed, but I was pretty sure I was still alive. Something inside me folded in on itself a hundred times. A hundred times would surely be enough.

I stood, resting a weary hand on a hedge for support and half falling into it for my efforts. My head was suddenly filled with a searing pain, like sharp metal was rattling around my skull. I closed my eyes to let it pass but it never truly did. The sky was betraying its gloom with a small slither of dawn at its edges. Somehow, the next day had found it in itself to come calling, and that allowed me enough inspiration to get walking. It was difficult; not least because I had no idea where I was or where I was going, but also because the sensation of walking now felt like walking in shoes made of sponge and I found myself wobbling erratically from side to side, teetering back into the hedgerow on more than one occasion. I bent down to take off my shoes and realised I wasn't wearing any. There was blood between my toes and one toenail had blackened. Like anyone educated in vanity, the sight repulsed me. It also confused me, as I had no recollection of taking off my shoes. That said, it was one amongst many memories that seemed to be being scattered behind me along the country lane, partly intentional, mostly uncontrollable.

I stumbled, bleary-eyed, into the nearest town. It was nowhere I recognised; places started looking the same a long time ago. This was just another anywhere with nothing and no one original. I stopped to rest on a small bench overlooking the centre, bathed in a streetlight that wouldn't go out, making the glazed sunlight just that little bit faker. I could hear the ever-present popping of gunfire and explosions on some faraway next-door horizon, and the air had a vague tinge of gunpowder about it, perhaps from fireworks, though probably not. A milk float was upended further down the street, snapped in two, it seemed, caved in to the street. Various cars lay dotted around, stripped of all but their muddy skeletons, some sitting charred, others smashed and dismembered. A shop alarm was going off somewhere, another impassioned plea for help that would never come.

I had nowhere to go, so perhaps, I thought, I should just stay where I was. I considered rooting out an old shop front to hide in, perhaps a house if I was lucky, but then what? I was devoid of inspiration, bereft of heart, and if the final curtain had been pulled at that very moment, I would have taken it with grace. There was nothing here any more. I still believed that things would change, things would heal, but realistically we had fallen so far that any repairs would be for a generation to undertake and I doubted I would ever see it through. I was all set to stretch out on the bench, close my eyes and wait, dream one last time and then let fate and fortune work themselves towards me when, as if desperate to still prove their worth, both did, instantly. It was a small voice, gently rocking me out of my pity and my dread, bringing me around and pulling me by the hand to the surface, and in that voice came a sound I wanted to cherish and repeat for eternity; it was the last time I ever heard innocence in anyone.

'S'cuse me missus, can you help me? I don't know where I am. I don't know what to do.' It was a young boy standing to my right, leaning in at me, staring with wide saucer-like eyes, the whites reddened, the pupils like massive ink stains. He was dressed in a tatty white t-shirt and khaki shorts, an oversized rucksack drooping down his back. I found myself saying, "the dear wretch, the dear sweet wretch," over and over in my head but kept the words quiet. Instead I just stared back. What a sight we must have been, two people staring at the other, bug-eyed and confused, each needing answers but only one adult enough to ask, 'Can you tell me where to go?'

'Where do you need to go, sweetheart?' I asked through a timid little cough, feeling blood at the back of my throat. I quickly swallowed it back and held my mouth. Looking at the young boy, I suddenly had an overwhelming urge for a mirror. I must have looked a state. This poor boy, confused and tearful, and this old hag his only hope, what a terrible thing. I rubbed at my nose and checked my palm for blood. My tongue ran around my lips, looking for cuts, and my hands quickly darted up to my hair, running themselves through the tatty heap, smoothing down the bits that weren't stiff with blood. He didn't seem scared, he didn't seem anything. He seemed frozen in both body and expression. Numbed to life.

'My mummy told me to get out and get safe. I don't know where to go. Where is safe?'

'Where is your mummy, sweetheart? Is she in trouble?'

'She's at home. People were hurting people. She said it wasn't safe. Where do I go?'

'What's your name? My name's Albie. What can I call you?'

'My name is Samuel. What does Albie mean?'

'It's short for Alberta.'

'My granddad is called Albert.'

'Is he? That's good.'

'Can you tell me where is safe, Albie? You're not going to hurt me, are you?'

'No, no of course I'm not, darling.' Those words snapped me and how I ever kept myself from crying I couldn't tell you. Perhaps on any other day it would have been impossible. I held out the palm of my right hand, gently spat on it, and asked him to do the same. Naturally he asked why, and politely pointed out I now had blood on my hand. 'Do you know what a pact is, Samuel?'

'No.'

'Never mind. It's like a promise. I'm making you a promise right here and now, okay? That promise is that I will never hurt you. Is that okay?'

'Mummy said adults are evil.'

'Not everyone is bad, Samuel. Like your mummy – she's not bad, is she?' He shook his head and slowly let his rucksack fall from his shoulder. 'Well, I'm like your mummy. I'm a good person too. And I promise I will never hurt you. And I promise I will make you safe.' I hated myself for saying those things; maybe I'm so used to lying and telling people what they want to hear that it's second nature now. Maybe the lie in me has a life of its own, rearing up and lashing out when I'm at my most vulnerable and desperate, and here there was, another victim of my bullshit. But what else did I have for him but a lie?

'She said that if I met a bad person I was to use this…' Samuel reached into his rucksack and pulled out a pistol the wrong way around, jabbing the butt towards my face. 'She has five of them, she said I could take this one.'

I gazed back at the butt of the pistol. Samuel was trying to muster a tough expression but succeeded only in looking like he was about to blub. I think from that moment I loved him, and I knew that I would do anything I could to make him safe, no matter what it took. I had nothing else to do, and nowhere else to go. Perhaps this was all that was left for me. He had caught me on a good day. I gently reached up to the butt of the gun, guided it around in his hand so the barrel was at me, then slowly lowered it and lifted it from his shaking hands.

'Can we go wherever is safe, Albie?'

'Of course we can, Samuel.'

I stood and led him by his hand, pocketing the pistol and desperately trying to think of where to go and what to do.

I kept off the main streets and roads, guiding Samuel first through an old car park and then into a small children's playground. I half expected him to want a go on the old and rusted swings, to ask me to push him high and fast, or perhaps to sit opposite him on the seesaw and scream deliriously, but he didn't. It was only once we had passed the swings and had set a path alongside an old duck pond that I realised it was me that had been having those thoughts, willing them on to him, wanting a moment of stupid fun to break through it all and let me forget where I was and that I was in charge; that I was an adult.

The duck pond spread out far and wide, breaking through feeble barriers into a lake that disappeared at the horizon like a corpse lip. I saw no ducks, I saw nothing on the dark water, nothing in it, and nothing around it; there was just Samuel and me, a rucksack and a pistol. Samuel was kicking up dust with his tiny trainers, and at one point he dribbled a balled burger wrapper and kicked it into the pond, punching the air victoriously and then looking at me, ashamed, as if forgetting himself and his surroundings for that second was the ultimate sin. He wrapped his hand back around mine and we kept walking. By this stage it was more him doing the leading. The pistol bounced in my coat pocket, the barrel gently prodding my ribs on occasion, reminding me it was there, constantly bringing the reality over any dared fantasy like a black veil. I wanted to toss it in to the pond. I had no knowledge of guns; had never shot one and would be more liable to scream in any situation where it was called for, and run away, than use it. But the gun belonged to Samuel, it was the young boy's gun and I left it where it was. I repeated that over in my head: "It's the young boy's gun, it's the young boy's gun…" and with each repetition I may just as well have fired a bullet in to my heart. What a fucking disgusting country we have made.

At a turn in the pathway, Samuel jerked my hand up

and pulled me towards a small bush, pointing with his free hand towards a grassy mound up ahead, lifting the pathway up and over it to some unseen destination. He could sense something and he was shaking again. I tried to steady him but I was shaking too; we pulled into the bush and crouched down. I fumbled my hand into my coat pocket and rested a hand over the butt of the pistol, praying that it wouldn't be necessary, daring to dream that the boy was blessed with a vivid imagination and confused senses and that whatever he imagined coming over that mound belonged in his head and nowhere else. We waited for several minutes. Time seemed to stretch like frayed elastic; I could hear his small breathing, could feel his tiny chest moving up and down slowly against my arm and in one discarded moment, against all logic, I found myself burying my face gently into his hair, wrapping him close, tighter than I should, pulling him in with one arm, desperate to protect him from everything and everyone. I yanked the pistol free and aimed it forward, scanning the distance with wonky sweeps of my arm, steadying it in my sweaty grip and hoping that nothing would come. Hoping I wouldn't have to be an adult.

A small van crested the mound and trundled down towards where we still hid. At first I didn't register it, was too scared to think of anything rational; the pathetic tinny tune it carried meant nothing to me either. It was Samuel that recognised it as an ice-cream van. As I looked back and saw the massive plastic ice-cream cone on its roof, I felt a little ashamed of myself. It's probably a good job that it will be Samuel's generation that fixes the country. I'm clearly past it.

Samuel jumped up quickly and was about to wave the van over when I pulled him down again to the bush and held a finger to his lips. He looked confused.

'We don't know if that's safe, Samuel. We have to be careful.'

'He's our ice-cream man. We buy ice-creams from him.'

'Yes, but it might not be safe.'

'Why?'

I had no reasonable answer to that besides the truth and I didn't think him ready or me that cruel. The tune still played from the van. It was falling into place in my memory slightly more by now; I knew it, had no doubt been irritated by it myself when I had been a child, but I had no name for it. The van stopped about thirty yards away from us and I could see a shape inside slide back the window and hover there, waiting.

'Can we get an ice-cream?'

'I don't know, Samuel.'

'He won't be here for long. He never stays long if people don't buy from him. He goes somewhere else then.'

I was stuck somewhere between desperately wanting this young boy to indulge in normality and me being terrified of reality. One more look at the disappointment and confusion on his face told me that I was going to go to the van for him, that I had to; it was just a question of how. I lifted myself up to the height of the bush and peered over. Samuel tried to do the same but I pushed him back. The pistol seemed to be gaining weight in my grip and I found, much to my distaste, my thumb stroking the hammer. I surveyed the area as best I could. We seemed very much alone. Certainly behind us we were safe, there was no one there, the lake was to one side and the other was just grass, a wide, open space, empty of people and threat. It was just that mound ahead, blocking my view and tantalisingly suggestive of what it may hide. I would just have to risk it; there was no way I could give disappointment to Samuel, somehow that was a given. No matter how stupid it was, I was going to get him an ice cream. I told Samuel to wait and push himself further back into the bush, get on all fours and don't move. He did it willingly. A game, perhaps, that's what he thought it was; I certainly hoped so. I turned my palm behind me, shielding the gun, and started walking.

The van was a dirty white and medicine pink. Mud had splattered the base, the tyres were balding and the whole van looked tired. As it loomed nearer, I noticed that the front window was cracked and the headlights were smashed. My heart started to plummet and my eyes stung in their effort to be alert to danger. The utter absurdity of the contradictions at play was very evident; I was getting an ice cream for a young boy and I was as terrified as I had ever been. I chanced a look back at the bush and could just make out Samuel's little face, poking out at the bottom. He waved at me as he met my stare. Gripping the pistol tight and bringing it forward to rest against my right leg, I let my left hand search for whatever loose change was in my pockets as I moved into view of the van window and found myself face to face with an old man dressed in a white jacket, a confusing multi-coloured fat-collared shirt underneath, demanding to be noticed. He leant forward into the window and leered down at me like last week's madman. Thick drool was at one corner of his mouth and there were flies in the window and in his hair.

'Well hello, young lady, what will it be?'

There is something both endearing and slightly perverted about being called a "young lady" when clearly the evidence in front of the person is not the case. It was obvious from the man's sloping body and elastic neck, craning his lunatic gait down to me, what was in evidence here. Even in these surroundings, I found it in me to pull up my top and hide my cleavage. Zach always used to call me a prude because I never liked to take my top off in bed and had paranoia about the fat on my thighs. Ordinarily I would have conceded to him that he may have had a point, but he never took his socks off in bed so I consider us even.

I tossed a handful of change onto the counter at the window and shifted to the side, away from the vulgarity in his face that was itching to be articulated. 'Whatever I can get for that, please. I don't care. Anything,' I said to him.

'I know you, don't I?' He said, ignoring the change. 'Sure I do. You're Albie aren't you?'

'I'm in a hurry, please just…'

'What you in such a hurry for? Got somewhere to go? I doubt that.'

'Says the man selling ice creams in a country that's killing each other.'

'What would you have me do? You and our beloved Prime Minister, what would your great wisdom be? I'm an ice cream man, what else should I be doing?'

'Please, just get me an ice cream, or whatever that money buys me…'

'That money don't buy you a bloodshot wink, bitch. You've got a fucking nerve walking these streets, don't ya?' He moved away from the window and I could hear him at the door to the van, wiggling the handle. He was mumbling violent words delivered in a stuttering wash of spittle. I turned around, ready to meet him at the door, and I suddenly realised that the pistol was already raised in my hand, my left hand cupped underneath for support, my thumb at the hammer again. Something unnaturally natural had invested me. I was screaming at my conscious self, berating it for what I must have looked like, but something had taken me over; I wanted him to face me, I wanted him to try and attack me. I wanted to kill him. There would be a time later on that the feeling would come back to me and I would drench myself in self-loathing and hatred, but at that moment, there was only one thing that mattered, and I had to be an adult about it.

As he rounded the front of the van, the craziness in his face was somehow magnified by the ice cream van and the colourful shirt, a contrast so sharp that it was a weapon of confusion, and for a brief moment, just in that one caught breath, he was somehow more of a threat than a hundred anarchists and murderers. Surprise seemed to slap him across the cheeks as he drew to me. I like to think that the sight of a gun in the hands of this pathetic bitch was what threatened to floor him, and perhaps for that split second it was, but before I had chance to even shout a warning, or to think of a warning to shout, I started to see where his surprise was really coming from. At that I joined the crazy mad bastard, watching helplessly as the real threat came creeping up to me like a rogue lover's tickling hands. I could sense, just out of my eyeline, just at the very edge – that creepy place where your demons sit watching – people moving out of the trees. Dark shapes were running at speed towards us and I swung around, away from the ice cream man, so quickly that my arm cracked against the wing mirror of the van and the pistol dropped to the floor. Pain flared in my wrist and shot up through my arm and then I screamed. It was Samuel I could hear first before the gunfire; he was calling my name and sprinting towards me, his stupidly small arms waving up and down as if he was trying to take off. I tried to call back at him but the words stuck in my mouth, and then came the pain in my head emanating outward and making my body limp and hollow. I remember falling and then I remember nothing until I woke up briefly in the back of a van, possibly the ice cream van, and my body was being bounced up and down like clothes in a washing machine as we trundled over rocky terrain. I was looking up at five hooded figures holding guns. I remember calling for Samuel and the figure in the middle stepping forward and leaning down to me.

'I know you! You're off the telly, aren't you?'

I rolled my head away and closed my eyes and everything stopped again.

It's remarkable how many people still recognise me from TV rather than politics. That says so much. I was famous, both Zach and I were mega, so I suppose it shouldn't be much of a surprise. There was a time when I ate that recognition up, lapping at every morsel, every connection and contact. It was so comfortable back then; I built a fake kingdom around me and I was never asked to step into reality and nor did I ever intend to. My world was all. I was a product that people bought and whilst people wanted me, I could do anything. That it would take me presenting reality TV to make the foul realities of life seep in and my love affair with TV to fade was an irony too ironic to believe.

I took the gig because of Zach. He had gone independent and it hurt me; it was the first time since we were together that he was offered anything without me and he didn't think twice. "Celebrity Abortion" a seven-week, five-nightly primetime show, a huge pay packet, exec producer credit and the promise of his own chat show. "Think of the money, Albie! We can convert the stables into a swimming pool! I can buy that water fountain of the Venus De Milo where the water comes out of the arm stumps and... Tropical fish, Albie! Tropical fish!" He was like a child asking to go play out with the rough gang of boys from up the street. I pitied him. I laughed at him. What could I do but tell him it wasn't my business what he did? He never really asked me if I minded – well he did, I suppose, after he'd told them he'd take it he was very careful to ask my opinion. So what was I to do but put myself on the market? I suppose I shouldn't have taken the first thing they offered me, but I was so desperate to show him that I mattered whether with him or without him. I sat on the job offer for five weeks before telling him. I was keeping it in reserve for our next argument.

I didn't think at the time that it was particularly radical. It was, to my mind, just the next logical evolution; it seemed like it was pretty much all that was left. They pitched it to me with the title and nothing more. Well, what more was necessary? "So You Want To Be Prime Minister?" It was a catchy title. The format, as it was explained to me, was as a quiz show, you know, test of intellect, oratory skills, knowledge of history and governmental practices and so on and so forth. But as these things tend to do it changed in pre-production and became a different beast; in this case, the talent show format that you will have seen on the TV. Zach was furious, of course, but when I hit him with it he didn't have a leg to stand on. We trounced "Celebrity Abortion" in the ratings and became the most watched show in thirty years.

It had to be done, that's what a whole raft of academics and great thinkers told us. People weren't voting and apathy had infested the country. The major parties were crumbling into minor irritations and the fringe parties were having a field day. There was a real danger that a few thousand votes were going to swing it to the big house for whoever could scrape them together and we could have ended up with anyone, any extremist loon that could talk louder and longer than the next; we could have slipped back generations. It was the biggest threat facing the country and something needed to be done.

Hindsight is a wonderful thing, of course. I have spent so long trying to justify it to people that the words are getting confused now. I know we did it with the best intentions, and even now I would take a fool over an extremist, but with everything that has happened the argument is hollow and it slips by people. They forget that they were the kingmakers and they are so quick to absolve themselves from blame. Aren't you? We made this situation; that's so easily put out of mind. His election was the highest vote turnout in generations. I say turnout, but I guess texting your vote from a sofa doesn't count as a turnout. We did it ourselves, don't you see? We made this, we created this, and now we have to ride out the storm. I've tried so hard to cling to my sanity in all that has unfolded. I'm a rational woman, and over the months I've clawed back a lot of what I shed to get to my false position of importance. If people get second chances then I want to make sure I'm ready for it. My greatest fear is that to find safety in this country you may also, now, have to befriend lunacy. That I should have to fall just that little bit further just so I can stand again terrifies me. I think of Zach in such moments; my beloved Zach who I helped speed down the road to ruin by my own selfish actions and scant regard. That he is probably now marked the very model of virtue and normality is the scariest thing of all. There is a leader in waiting if ever there was. Not that he'd get my vote. I think, from here on in, with a polite nod to suffragette, sisterly solidarity, I will abstain in future.

Zach and I had drifted apart long before Archie did

what he did. We had been having problems for as long as I can remember; I just got used to never articulating them to anyone, so scared I was that they'd be the final nail in the career coffin. We were Albie and Zach... Zach and Albie... Zalbie, that peculiar one-headed media beast that some lazy halfwit coined and ran with. If I had known that he would have dropped out at the first independent offer, I would never have stayed the support for as long as I did. That he was a drunk was fairly well known; he used to leak the stories of his rehab visits whenever he hadn't been in the papers for a month and I would go with him, the dutiful wife, and we would smile for photos, arm in arm. I would give them some variation on our theme and would do what I needed to keep it alive whilst he was inside. The pills and potions he was taking were less well known. That was my fault, I talked him into it, but what was I supposed to do? When you come home and your husband is having a row with an empty space, you really should do something.

To see how he was chipped away at me in small brittle pieces. It was horrible. He would promise to sort himself out for me, I would tell him not to invest in me, he would fail and then the next week we would have the same conversation. Round and round we went, never getting anywhere, save the place we started, which was the last place either of us wanted to be. I should have left him long ago, before I did what I did and had the chance to destroy him; that was the last thing I wanted. It was Archie that talked me in to staying with him. He pleaded with me to remain constant for him, make him feel I was still obtainable, which considering what Archie and I were up to together seems incredibly cruel. But the intention was meant to be good. Archie always said that Zach would go under without me, and he was right. Whether Archie really wanted his friend to stay sane or whether he just liked the excuse to keep our affair secret is open to debate. He is a bastard so anything is possible. I wonder how history will judge Archie? A footnote on how low our country stooped, or just another guy who couldn't get it right? Either way, he will still be happy he's being talked about. Perhaps in the future they can remake this present with a Hollywood ending. He'd like that; he'd consider all this madness worthwhile. Prime Minister Archibald Butcher, our beloved marionette leader.

I came to in a child's bedroom, my first waking sight being wallpaper decked out in cartoon characters I was just too old to place. I was in bed against a wall of impossibly fluffy pillows and I remember thinking that I wanted it to be like that for ever. I wanted to freeze that feeling and wear it like a coat. It was like waking up from a beautiful dream and trying to hold it against reality, trying to urge yourself back to sleep just for another minute of it. There was to be no more dreaming then, though. I was awake and scared. The room smelt of urine and neglect and I had a headache from nail to follicle. A glass of milk was on a small bedside table next to me and a small man in a hood was sat at the opposite end of the room. He waved at me as I sat up and ushered me to the milk. Drinking it dry and wiping away my milk moustache, I just sat watching him, unable to even ask the inevitable. I noticed some clean clothes had been left at the base of the bed and the man nodded me to them and stood and turned his back. It was a good five minutes before I even stepped out of bed, let alone dressed, but in all that time he didn't move, didn't turn, didn't say anything. One last gentleman perhaps, I thought, or maybe just one more person scared of human beings. I hoped for the former; I expected the latter.

When I was dressed and blessedly wearing shoes again, the man opened the bedroom door and led me out through a small kitchen and out of the front door. It was only once out into a huge stairwell that I realised we were in a tower block. Looking down, I guessed we were on the fifth floor. The man started walking upwards then stopped and turned back to me, speaking in a soft low voice, almost apologetic and frightened to break the silence. 'It's the seventeenth floor we need, will that be okay for you? Can you make it?'

'Sure,' was all I had to offer.

We began to climb. On the fourteenth floor,

someone had written in black paint along one wall, it read, "AND THEN CAME THE STRANGER". Two floors further on, the same hand in the same paint had simply written, "OH". On the next turn of the stairwell, my feet slapped down hard onto shattered concrete and something flew from under my new shoes and fell down the stairwell. There was an iron gate at the entrance to the next floor and a small box was attached just above the handle. It looked like some sort of intercom. Razor-sharp wire ran in scatty curls across the top. Glass had been embedded on the top rim of the gate just underneath the wire. In small letters just above the letterbox it read, "NO COLD CALLERS". The man pressed the intercom and waited.

'Are you okay?' He asked me.

I nodded.

A voice with all the comfort of a bent fork in a broken heart came from the intercom, making the man jump: 'Yes?'

'It's me,' the man whispered into the intercom.

'Yes,' the voice said. It was a horrible voice, the sort of voice that talks to you from underneath your bed. The gate clicked open a fraction. 'Enter,' the voice said. We did.

This floor was scattered with rubbish. Four of the flats on this level were doorless and dimly lit. The fifth at the far end had a door, a dark blue door, lit from a small light above it. As we approached, it opened wide and a man stepped out. He was bony and tall, like a tree growing out of the floorboards. He welcomed us with a smile of chipped china and let one long twig arm usher us forth into his flat.

The flat was stripped of all mod cons and most furniture. A sofa sat against one wall and a small rickety rocking chair opposite it was next to a large map pinned to a noticeboard. Ripped curtains hung over the windows. One was boarded up, another had holes in it stuffed up with torn-up cereal packets. There was warmth in the flat but I felt unbearably cold, the heat serving only to cook out the smell of piss and hopelessness. The human twig man swept into the flat and swung himself dramatically onto the rocking chair. At his side stood two more people, their hoods pushed up their heads. In the meagre light I could just make out their faces – the light was enough to reveal their age – and my shock was still generous enough to show itself when I realised these were old people. Old enough to be my parents. That's old enough. The man who had escorted me in sat on the sofa and patted the empty space next to him. He took off his hood and I saw he was more my age, but that's still pretty old. I thought of Samuel at this showing of age; I wanted to turn to the man in the rocking chair, the man clearly in charge of whatever was left here, and ask him where he was, but somehow there was nothing in me to articulate. I found myself shrugging and sitting on the sofa. The man on the rocking chair crossed his ridiculous legs and I was put in mind of two snakes in a love tryst. There was a long silence in the room. Each pair of eyes scrutinised me, searching me out, and somewhere a loud clock was ticking but it sounded like it was stuck. The trapped sound was a reassuring rhythm, echoing out, asking instead of telling.

'You have questions?' The stick man said, his vulgar twigs of fingers strumming his root stump chin. 'Yes?'

I shrugged then nodded.

'You are very welcome. I am Charles. I am the head of the Apricot Avenue neighbourhood watch and today you are to witness a revolution. The suppression of decency and British values will begin to end this very day and in this very place. We sit in the centre, the very beating heart of our own creation of hell, and we shall start the long process of dragging us all back into the light. We shall fight the flames of destruction with our own fire and we will not cease until the evil we have created is scorched out of our world. This country will be born again anew, free of defilement and filth, corruption and decadence, and we here in this room shall be the founding fathers of the next generation.'

'Lovely place you have here,' I said.

'It is vile. We have vermin. The walls breath death. But it is where we will begin again. You must cleanse the badness to achieve goodness. You shall be witness, Albie. You oversaw one revolution, now you may see how it should be done. Your place in history will be assured.

You will have been there at the end and there at the beginning of the new age. You will straddle history. Gods have done less.'

'I have somewhere to be.'

'Yes. Here.'

'Well, no…'

'Do you believe in revolution?' Charles asked.

'I have a slight conflict of opinion when it comes to that. I see its merits but it seems to me that most people I have met that espouse its virtues are arseholes.'

'You were born in TV, Albie. Those people do not exist. Reality has yet to wrap its arm around you.'

'I dunno, it's been hugging close these last few months.'

'It is good to question people. We all must question and demand. But we must also follow what we believe to be right. Mustn't we?' Charles leaned forward to me and his face looked slightly demented in the low light of the room. 'I never voted for Archie. Somehow it seems important to tell you that,' he said with a cold sigh that iced the room. The people at his shoulder seemed to move at his voice, seemed to want to follow his words as they floated around the room. He had them enthralled and held there at whim. That he had a god complex was not the greatest fear I felt; it was the willing corruption that made it so easy for him that teased out the biggest questions and suggested the most frightening answers.

'I didn't vote for him either, Charles.'

This seemed to amuse him greatly and he uncoiled his legs and stretched, slowly easing himself out of the rocking chair, and stood to his full height, shy of the ceiling by nothing more than a laboured thought. 'Stand a moment, Albie. Let me show you something,' Charles crossed the room to a window and waited for me. I raised myself up and half walked, half waddled to the window and stood next to him. The view was awful and there was miles upon miles of it to see from this high up.

'I despair of this country. I really do. There is so much potential, but we have fallen down a crack somewhere along the line and don't seem in a hurry to get out,' Charles said into the windowpane. 'People always say there is good and bad everywhere. Tell me what you see, Albie. Social dysfunction, the apathetic generation, laziness, crime... It's not just us, I know, but when did it all get so damn dirty?'

'Is this the point where you tell me it wasn't like that in your day?'

'But it wasn't Albie, it really wasn't... And I say this as a child of the war.'

'Which one?'

'The one with the nice uniform.'

'You believe it far more sporting that we fight other nationalities rather than our own?'

'It was supposed to protect our way of life. Look what we have done with it.' Charles took a large pair of binoculars from a hook on the wall next to the window and handed them to me. 'Tell me what you see.'

I took the binoculars from him and looked out. It seemed to me, from up there, like a child's model village that had been trampled on by a clumsy adult foot. Once proud, imposing and phallic buildings were smashed and flattened. The streets were empty bowling alleys with scattered pins dotted around, the horizon pulsing spots of orange under the heavy fug that lay on it like a fat spent lover. Charles reached to the binoculars and gently pushed them downwards.

'Look down, Albie.'

Below us, a car park seemed to circle the base of the tower block. Charred black cars sat around like giant turds and running amongst them were small figures, ants, insects, flies…

'Vermin,' Charles said into my ear, a deathly whisper that seemed to pass right through my head and die at the wall next to me. 'Young vermin; the worst sort. The young don't resign themselves to being vermin and believe they are invincible. They live to infest and irritate. You ever see an old, fat, rat, cornered in a room? It longs for you to pick it up and kill it.'

'When you say young…'

'Children. Yes. But I'm an old man, Albie; to me, children are children to eighteen. I weep at the speed children grow up these days. So desperate they are to shed childish wallowing and take up adult indulgences. There's nothing so great about being an adult. Why would they not cling to youth for as long as society lets them?'

'I had a boy with me when…'

'When we saved you from the ice cream man?'

'Saved me?'

'He was going to kill you.'

'How do you know?'

'It's my job to know. It's my job to protect those that need protecting. Those that deserve it.'

'I deserve it?'

'You're a different beast, Albie. I don't pretend to sit in judgement on you. I don't believe what I see on the television, but whether you deserve it or not it was decided that was what would happen. I found the irony of making the ringmaster of our downfall the witness to our new creation quite delicious. The boy is safe. He is downstairs colouring in a colouring book.'

The "ringmaster" comment cut to my core but I didn't pick Charles up on it. Somehow, all argument looked likely to fall off him like water off a stone statue; there was a world created in this tower block, there were players, there was an order and there was an audience. I was trapped in another person's show of vanity, a man sat astride his plastic kingdom with a hard-on and some serious delusions. There was only one question that seemed to matter, only one I felt able to ask: 'Did he ask after me?'

'The boy? Yes, I believe he did.'

'May I see him?'

'There will be a time for such things. Take a look at this estate, Albie. It is not something rare and unworldly. It is quite typical. When the country fell, such places as this became weeping sores. Easy places for the disease to infest and breed. We've always had crime on this estate, drugs of course, much of that, muggings, beatings, arson, had a rape last year... We've not had many murders, though. As a watch group, we have always been quite proud of that. In the first week after what happened, there were twenty-five murders. Flats were burned out. People displaced. Men, women, children – it was a nightmare so thick it choked this estate. In such circumstances, of course, in times of anarchy and chaos, people rise to take advantage, and from such abject chaos tinpot dictators are born. Power will never be unimportant to the human race – I don't need to tell you that, of course.'

'I've never had power, never wanted it.'

'Dear me, dear, you say it with such conviction I believe you really do think it. You are mistaken, of course. But then maybe it was never for you to see it. We at Apricot Avenue let our guard down just long enough to let the evil in. We showed weakness and the weak must now become the strong. Our new dictator was a sixteen-year-old child, a boy born into criminality and viciousness and a boy that saw his opportunity and took it. When the police stopped coming round here, when there was no recourse to his actions, he and those at his bidding took this place by the throat and created themselves a little empire. Today we take that away from them. Do you think they will put it on television?'

I looked at Charles and then back into the room at those that hung from his creation like dying men hold on to the last air of a sealed room. The irony, the joke of his story of a sixteen-year-old king of violence hadn't escaped me and I almost pitied those people around me for their delusions, but then this is what we had become; kings of a castle whose drawbridge was down and whose defences were exposed. Who was I to highlight the hypocrisy, to belittle one man's perceived wisdom? I just wanted to be far away, and I wanted to see Samuel.

Charles wrapped a bony arm around my shoulder and hugged me to him. 'This is the corruption of society Albie. The police, government, and the law... Everything is failing us. They have left us alone and yet we are failing each other. Do you not want to fight to change things for the better?'

'No.'

'Then what do you want?'

'I want to be away from here. I want to leave. Samuel and I must leave and go somewhere else.'

'Where else is there?'

'There must be somewhere out there where we can –'

'Be safe? But what are you prepared to do to ensure that? This is our home, are we not supposed to fight for it? I've lived here thirty years; others longer. Why should we leave? Most of us are old. I've no desire for new things, new places; I've travelled the world, seen many great things, and now I just want to see out my days in the place I have chosen to live. With my friends. With those I care for. I had no longing for what has happened to this country...'

'Are you sure?'

'Why would you say such? You make me sound a monster. You think I enjoy this?'

Yes, I did. But what would have been the point in saying it? I was talking to the brainwashed and the deluded, drunk on power and living one last fantasy to make them feel alive and worthwhile. I looked to the noticeboard, the map; I saw photos and diagrams, plans and rotas. It was a war room and Charles a dedicated General, his foot soldiers compliant and willing. The astonishing detail, the grand scale plan of attack, all there on the noticeboard was terrifying. Somehow the casualness of recent horrors paled into juvenile acts alongside what I had obviously just walked in to. Back behind the binoculars, I looked down once again and saw figures gathering at the base of the tower block. Ten, twenty, fifty, could have been a hundred; the insects swarmed into one large, huddled mass. Someone amongst them carried a flaming torch and there was screaming and bellowing from the car park like the battle cry of savages. Charles turned to the room and simply nodded; the people left the room at speed and from the floor below I could hear fists banging on doors, people calling to their neighbours, voices gathering on the stairwell and I looked back to Charles, looking for something to reassure me that this nightmare was not real, but what I saw clamped around me like steel jaws. Charles was standing before the window an old army helmet on his head and a rifle swung over one shoulder.

I had met mad people before of course, my dear, dear Zach being exhibit A – in fact, I seem to attract them – but with Charles the madness seemed to have spun full circle and come back to him as normality. "Mad is bad," my father used to say, "but if you see a madman with power then lock your chastity belt and run for the hills." That was all I had left. That and Samuel.

'Tonight, we make a stand and take back this part of England. Tomorrow, anything will be possible. You can sit or you can fight, but you will bear witness, Albie. History will embrace you.'

'I want to see Samuel.'

'Then do.'

That, it seemed, was the end of the conversation. Charles extended a long hand to me. I shook it and hoped that it wouldn't break off. Charles led me back out of the front door, stopped at the first doorless flat and held an arm out to the main gate. I hovered at the flat door and chanced a look inside. It was too dark to see anything much but I could just make out a stack of what looked like crates at one end.

'Don't go in there, please.'

'Why, what's in there?'

'That's the armoury.' There was not even a hint of humour in his voice despite how much he seemed to enjoy saying that. 'We have been preparing for this day for a long time. We have the will and the means to level this place. And if we do, we have the heart to rebuild it.'

'Revolution?'

Charles nodded and held his arm out again to the main gate. 'It has to start somewhere. Glad we met you, Albie. Enjoy the show.'

I hobbled down the stairs. People were filling out the stairwell, old people were carrying pots and pans, rolling pins and kitchen knives. Someone was beginning a chant. A woman with a blue rinse and varicose veins was loading a machine gun. The passageways were blocked, choked with feverish excitement and nervous chatter. I began looking in the first flat I came to, walking through room after room, searching for Samuel, calling to him, turning over furniture and pushing past people. It was the fifth flat I found him in and he greeted me with a smile and proudly showed me his colouring-in book. I wanted to collapse in tears but held them at bay as I scooped him up in my arms and headed out of the door, once more not having the first clue where I was going.

We got down to the tenth floor before the first

explosion rocked the tower block. At this, we all seemed to shift sideways. I fell with Samuel in my arms, rolling over expertly and making sure we landed on my back. He seemed excited by it all, peering up to the stairwell windows – looking for fireworks, perhaps. It was just as well, as I had no ability to tell him the truth even if I had got a handle on it. Perhaps Charles had been right about youth, if not about much else; perhaps it was a sin of society that children were forced to speed through to adulthood, bypassing innocence and wonder so as to be burdened by the weight of disappointment. I tried to think of ways to turn it in to a game for Samuel. Did children still play Cowboys and Indians these days? I doubted it, but decided that that would be my tack. I managed a laugh, a gentle whooping sound, as the first gunshots met each other. I'm good at being fake, it was my job for so many years, and I can do that; I did it then and I did it well. I think he even enjoyed himself. I was careful to turn him away from the blood, shield his ears to the loudest of explosions and the coarsest of words. I knew that I could create a little world for him whilst getting him out. I create worlds. We all do, I suppose. Charles and I, all of us, we are all so intrinsically moulded together by fantasy and ego, but I do it better than anyone else. I'm a professional.

'Exciting, isn't it?' I said gently into Samuel's ear as the stairwell windows on the ninth floor blew inwards and the rain shards peppered our hair. An old man charged past us, waving a frying pan above his head and bellowing vicious promises of retribution through a war-painted face. 'Goodies versus baddies. We are the goodies – right Samuel?'

'We're the good guys! Yeah!'

'That's right.'

'What do we have to do?'

'We have to find a car.'

'Can I have my mummy's pistol?'

'No, darling, you don't need that.'

'Who are all these people? Are these the good guys too?'

'Oh yes, darling, we are all the good guys. Come on...'

The words stuck in my throat. I pulled him closer for comfort, my comfort; the softness of his hair against my cheek may as well have been as harsh as a metal brush for the comfort it gave. His young smell, too; that soft and gentle odour at his neck and face just made the contrast more brutal. I wedged him further up my body and told him to hold on tight. Further down the stairwell, the mass of bodies was growing thicker, bodies charging downwards, bodies charging upwards. Those that had met in the middle were wildly hitting and striking each other. Contorted looks of viciousness and joy all blended together in one morphing ugly portrait of human failings. To our side, two men were firing shots from the window, firing empty, reloading and firing clean again, rigid and robotic and set in their task, their desire. Out of the window I could see small objects falling; cutlery, a television, a chair, what looked like Charles' rocking chair at one point, and then, like black, oversized hail, what could only have been hand grenades. I pushed us against one wall of the stairwell, wrapped my arms tight around Samuel and waited for the explosion. When it came, belching forward and inwards in a series of hefty bangs, those of us on the stairwell tumbled forward en masse, some falling over the banisters, some holding onto those they were fighting for support, others just sucked under the stampede of feet, disappearing into the blur of bodies. We fell against a young man and a woman, two people I had seen further up the stairwell less than five minutes ago, and they turned to us and began lashing out, blind to threat or friend, unaware and uninterested who we were or what we wanted. I turned Samuel from them and let them rain their aggression onto my back and sides, gently cheering in to Samuel's ear, making it seem like I was excited by the game and joyous to be a participant, all the while hoping that he was young and naïve enough for me to get away with the lie. I secretly knew that, deep down, no one is that innocent these days, even those we hopefully bestow innocence on.

Someone started firing down the stairwell and the surge of people suddenly seemed to narrow, arching away from the bullets like a river separating over rock or rubbish. The two who had been attacking me had suddenly gone, their fickle anger caught elsewhere or blown out – who could say? I certainly didn't care. I stood to a crouch and started pushing myself between bodies, tumbling forwards sometimes, skidding down steps on my knees, the hand shielding Samuel's head from battering against bodies. Some people fell; I could hear the clanking as some thudded against the banisters. The dull thuds that followed those that fell all the way to the bottom were the worst sounds I had ever heard. I still hear them now; I probably always will. I got to the next landing, already having lost count of which floor I was at, and ducked into the nearest flat, rolling us over onto the floor and releasing Samuel into the kitchen as I lay there, my laboured breathing catching against something broken in my chest – something even more fragile than my heart.

Samuel was up on the kitchen worktop in a flash and staring down at the mayhem playing out in the car park. I heard him say "wow" to himself, his hands pressed against the windowpane and his eyes gobbling up everything they could find. I eased myself up and stood and wrapped an arm around him, pulling him away from the window.

'Don't touch the glass, Samuel, it might break.'

'Everyone's fighting.'

'Yes, I know. Cowboys and Indians, isn't it?'

'It's not, though, is it? My mummy told me that

people were hurting each other on purpose because they could. Is that true?'

'No, Samuel, of course not.'

'It is, isn't it? You're biting your lip. Mummy always bites her lip when she knows something she doesn't want me to know.'

'We have to get out of here, Samuel.'

'Find a car!'

'Yes, find a car and get out of here.'

'Are they going to hurt us?'

'No. I won't let them, Samuel. I promise.'

'Okay then.'

I left Samuel rooting through the kitchen cupboards, idly chatting to himself, and stared from the window. We must have been about seven floors up. The mass of people in the car park was much easier to see now, there was some definition, and they were individual shapes rather than one horrid swarm. People were running in and out of the car shells, surges of bodies were flooding the entrance of the tower block; occasionally, one or two bodies fell to their knees or buckled backwards as more gunfire broke the sky. I thought of Charles up there overseeing the carnage; I imagined him standing at the window, casually dropping hand grenades and stretching himself proudly to his full and considerable height. Was he having fun? Almost certainly he was. Outside the flat, a blast of gunfire tore through the stairwell and the door shredded inwards, punched through with an immediate fury. I grabbed Samuel and dragged him from the kitchen and across to the living room, which was as far from the front door as we could get. He was starting to cry, my feeble pretence of it being a game no longer standing up to a child's scrutiny. Once more, I found myself trying to find the reassuring lie for a frightened male. Was Samuel so very different from Zach? Even if Samuel, at his tender age, had more chance out there in this world, the weight of responsibility was no less heavy. I found myself thinking back to Zach. The cold, callousness of his parting words to me had been apparent, hidden under the dreadful truth he had discovered about Archie and me. I had found myself telling him I didn't love him any more, anyway; that I was going to leave him as well, pathetically trying to get some foothold in my pride and deflect blame. I told him that I was scared and that I didn't understand what was happening, just that I didn't want it to be a reality for me. How arrogant I was to think that I could be free of this whilst others had no choice. That's TV for you, fame and celebrity; that's being told you were special and that you mattered, that you were somehow better than the average man or woman. I lived willingly with the delusions and encouraged them. I thought again of Charles and knew that we really weren't that far removed. I thought of Archie and felt dirty, then of Zach's remarkable casualness about it all. He said he had had time to absorb the truth of it all because he had been watching it on TV. I was mortified and embarrassed before I was ashamed. He offered to show me the footage and I wanted to hit him. Of course, I put the blame on Archie; even then, at that point in my life, I found myself spitting lies out like they were a passing fashion to be worn out. But he did not shout or scream; he just sat there waiting for me to leave, not listening, or if a word in ten crept in, he was choosing not to understand them. He had packed a few bags for me and said he would put the kettle on whilst I packed the rest. The thing that always stays with me about that moment was Zach's absolute unwillingness to see Archie in that image. It was as if the person he had seen with his wife was not his dear friend and leader but a total stranger, someone nameless and imagined. When I mentioned Archie's name, Zach just smiled and nodded and spoke about how difficult a job Archie had, about the lawyers and the speech he must give, about the lies and half-truths that had put us in such a perilous situation. He seemed to shift persona at every mention of Archie's name, over-elaborating their friendship and never once referring back to what he used to be. It was as if Archie, his friend, had been born the moment he took office and Archibald Butcher, plumber, was an entirely separate person; someone who could be hated with ease, perhaps? I worried what would happen when the reality aligned itself with the truth and he finally embraced the knowledge of what we had done. I didn't know what

Zach was capable of. Zach is a good man but I have no idea what a good man does when given justification to be bad. Even in our current carnival he would surely never apply.

I felt dizzy and weak. Hatred swept me and painted me and I hugged Samuel tighter at each stroke. I hoped that Zach was living a life amongst all of this. There was a part of me, probably always will be, that wanted him to come charging in and save me, to have sought me out and declared his love again, despite the facts against it, but he never would. As soon as I could, I would make it so that he would never find me again, so that no one would find me – or Samuel. There was something better out there; there had to be. "There's always something on the other channels, Alberta," my father used to say, and he was a wise man.

I don't know where I'm going to go but I suspect it doesn't really matter, does it Zach? You're hard to talk to, do you know that? So hard to have a conversation with. Random words and touches... That's what we've been doing. There are times when you have scared me. I look at you now and I'm not sure that you are the same person. I hope you are taking your medication... I hope you are looking after yourself... I hope... I wish good things to you, Zach. I hope you have some normality. It's what we all need, Zach, normality; I thought I had it but it was a sham. We both know it. I've stepped from sham to sham so many times that I forgot what reality was.

But I know now Zach and it isn't this. They aren't going to make a TV show from it, believe me.

Do you remember what you said to me when we first met, that thing about verses and choruses? Do you remember that, Zach? How people always remember choruses to songs before they remember the verses? You said that the world could be divided into verses and choruses; those who make an impact and are remembered, and the rest of us – most of us – who don't. I wonder if you still think that, Zach? I wonder if you still crave one over the other? I wonder, Zach… I do and that's why I have to step out of this madness. I hope you understand, Zach. Be safe.

I went through the cupboards in the living room looking for things I could use. "Getting tooled up" is the phrase Samuel used and I was quick to tell him that he was wrong, but I couldn't quite find a more accurate description. I wrapped an old blanket from the top of the sofa around my waist for extra padding and protection, tearing a few strips off so that Samuel could have the same. We both fastened it tight around each other with some string he found in an old bureau. He picked up a paperweight in the shape of an elephant, an old letter opener (which I was quick to relieve him of) and an old hockey stick that lay unloved in one corner, bound together with thick tape and hope. I tore some stuffing from the sofa and draped it over Samuel's head, tying string around it and then under his chin, making it the most ridiculous hat ever created. He seemed to find it funny until he caught sight of himself in a mirror and his face sagged. I hurried him on. We collected curtain rails, snapping them in two so we could have one each. I tied a third to the hockey stick for extra strength. I darted back into the kitchen and gathered up some old rusty knives. None looked to be able to penetrate anything, but there was something repugnantly reassuring about holding them. I gripped one and jammed the rest, handle-down, into my belt. Samuel was getting nothing more dangerous than the hockey stick. Just outside the kitchen was an old hat stand and tucked in to the bottom of it was an old orange umbrella. I swiped it and brandished it in front of me like a sword. It was all that was left. I rejoined Samuel and we gathered our things. I ran through what we should do, making everything up as I went along and trying hard to sound like a responsible adult, and all the while Samuel picked at his hat and scuffed his shoes on the threadbare carpet. He nodded with each instruction and I simply had to hope that he was listening and taking it in. I would keep him away from as much as I could, but I knew there may come a time when the roles might have to be reversed. Outside, in the stairwell, another surge of people pressed down on the encroaching invaders and a young man with a face of undiluted confusion seemed to be carried along on top, crowd surfing between the waves of people. The gun in his hand may just as well have been a stick of rock.

I took Samuel to the door, standing against the wall and peering through into the stairwell, waiting for enough of a break in the people to give us a fighting chance. I gripped Samuel's hand and he squeezed it back. I looked down at him, holding his hockey stick and scratching his foam hat, and I found myself wondering about his mother, about her seeming ease at letting him go, pistol in rucksack, to fend for himself. How bad had it got there? How many scars had it left on him that were yet to show through? It was the first time, that very moment in the doorway that the weight of responsibility started to lift. At that moment I would have done anything for him without even coercion of thought. It had become instinct. A mother's instinct.

There soon came a small break in people and I swung Samuel into it quickly and he started hitting out with the hockey stick, wild whooshing movements. The stick broke almost instantly on the wall but he kept on with the end that was left. I slapped an approaching man with the curtain rail, swung it back and then out in front of me, darting circles in the air like a magic wand ordering back the oncoming hoards. I brought the umbrella into play at the next landing; it was strong and sturdy. I poked and stabbed, hit and whipped with it, I struck so many people, but still that orange umbrella kept hold. Samuel kept one hand on my belt (the side away from the knives) as I had told him, as we went down to the next landing. I continued striking with the umbrella in one hand and the rusty knife in the other. I caught a woman in the ribs with the brolly and bedded the knife into one man's shoulder. The man spun round as the dull pain flashed through him and I saw that it was the hooded man who I had seen on waking in the child's bedroom. He looked mortified as he saw me and pretty soon he was lunging at me, his big fists clenched to beat me, batter me down and kill me. He managed to push Samuel and I apart and Samuel went for him with the nub of the hockey stick. The man had me at the railings, his hands round my throat, pushing me back, trying to topple me over, when an explosion shattered the entrance to the tower block. A fireball punched through just beneath us and the force lifted us off our feet. The stairwell seemed to bend forward and suddenly a giant hole had been blown through the wall and we were arching up and towards it. The floor above us seemed to be melting, concrete and rubble pouring down the long throat of the stairwell, ready to spit out of the mouth in the wall and down onto the car park below. I tried, in that instance, to look for Samuel, but everything was a blur. I saw just a passing flash of colour and legs, and then I was falling in a small shower of dust and darkness, down through the hole and into the night, the chilling breeze a pincushion at my back as I tumbled and landed with a cold thud on to a small flowerbed next to the car park. Everything shut down for a minute. I knew something had shattered in my arm, I knew that if

I looked at it I would see something incorrect and ugly, so I turned away, instead looking across the flowerbed at the car park, and the passing feet and legs that poured past me. I was, finally, ignored.

I could see Samuel's face everywhere, even in the oppressive light cast by the stone-choked sky that was flecked with streaks of sunset like rivers of blood; the burnt cars, the neglected flowerbed, he was everywhere and in all and I wanted to cry for him. I felt part of me had been torn free and burnt as I watched, the pain of my imagination and love rendering any breaks and cuts the most minor irritation. I thought of him alone amongst the waves of hatred and violence coursing through the tower block, a stupid foam hat and half a hockey stick, and I could only hope the compassion and humanity of any random soul, standing between him and death.

I could hear a noise over my shoulder and I turned to see the hooded man, the knife still in his shoulder, lying next to me. His face was bloodied and ugly but still somehow showed him to be my age, maybe younger. He was mouthing something to me, reddened lips struggling to form anything but a stupid gurgle. I think he was trying to call me a bitch. I don't know. I just stared back and watched him as he tried to rise, as he fell back and then tried again. His hands were still trying to clench and if he had anything left to give, I knew he was going to give it to me. I simply didn't care at that point. He could have killed me and I probably would have let him. Samuel had been the reason to hold on and get out. Without the reason, I may as well just let the curtain fall. As the man took his fifth attempt at standing, he suddenly lurched at me and I felt some of the blood from his lips strike me. His eyes bore the most understandable sort of madness and I knew that this was it. I made peace with it in that moment. It was okay, I thought, not ideal, but okay. There was a disappointment that I would go this way, in this most ungracious fashion, but I knew that no one was watching, so why should I care? He seemed to find strength from somewhere, I could see it in his face; the gritted teeth and fractured smile, the veins at his neck straining as he conjured up every last ounce of fury he had left. I just smiled at him and waited. He didn't lunge again, though; indeed for a moment he didn't even move. He seemed to just freeze in time and space, and then, with a dreadful sigh like thick gloop draining down a plughole, he tumbled backwards and stared up at the sky. I didn't understand it and didn't question it until I saw the elephant-shaped paperweight lying in the grass next to him and my heart spun upside down and threatened to implode. I yanked myself round and screamed as the break in my arm moved bone where it didn't want to be. I looked up and there he was – my dear Samuel, foam hat on head, half a hockey stick slung over his shoulder and a look of feverish determination on his face. He moved to me with a slow confidence and offered me his hand. I could not have been prouder of him.

I hope you will forgive any vagueness from this point. I cannot escape with the truth. We got out of that place and found another, then two more. It was Samuel that found the car, some small thing with the keys still hanging in the ignition. It was a miracle, I suppose. I took a few minutes wiping the blood away from the upholstery before I let Samuel get in. He sat on the kerb, playing with the hockey stick nub and chatting to himself. I drove, with no small amount of difficulty because of my arm, my legs, my back, my every damn thing, until the petrol tank emptied and then we walked some more. We found a place, a nice little place, and it feels safe. As safe as I've felt in many years. Samuel seems happy with it and that matters more than anything. He doesn't ask after his mother, doesn't ask questions as to what went on and threatens to continue to do so. He just takes it in his stride and I am jealous of that. He spends a lot of time playing by himself as I sleep a great deal. My injuries make it difficult to get around much. I've attended to what I can, but some things are going to need professional help, should there be any professionals out there, or even someone willing to help. I'm trying not to let Samuel know about my wounds; he has no need to know that we must soon set off again just because I am falling apart. He's happy here, and every moment here that I allow him, I feel good. I could build a life for us here, I think; there is certainly the potential. How long we would be granted this sanctuary is of course impossible to say, but then who can or ever could say such with any assurance? There are no rules any more, nothing definite or obvious. We are making it up as we go along. Was that not how it always starts? It is just about the instinct of the moment now and my instinct, carefully arrived at over several months, is telling me to keep safe. There really is nothing else any more. Wherever Archie is, he will have to fend for himself; he's good at attending to himself. Zach must also not be a consideration, as hard as that is; I just can't afford it. I hope he understands and I hope he doesn't hate me. More than anything, I just hope that he doesn't come looking for me, as I could relent. Love will do that. Love will do almost any crazy fucking thing.

I seem to forever be thinking about what Zach used to say about verses and choruses. Those of us who shout loud enough to be remembered and those that hide well enough so they aren't. We always used to crave one over the other. Perhaps it was our downfall. Perhaps it was the falling rock that started the collapse, I don't know. My father would know, in fact I'm sure he would have an opinion on it all. He would be quick to tell us all where we went wrong. My father once told me that it's often better to have people unaware of your flaws than to have the world privy to your achievements. I'm not entirely sure what he meant by that, but he was an astute man so I guess there is something to be read from it. But in the end, they are just words, aren't they? It's easy to set the world right from an armchair. In that world, he was the last great eminent thinker of his age. That was enough to make him happy.

Archie's Verse

In the beginning…

It was reality and reality made sense, people lived it and thought nothing of it. Then, at some point when we weren't looking, reality became a dream to chase and we've been pushing past each other to get to it ever since. I used to be important. I used to be the most important person in every room. Now I'm just the voice of other people's words, the acceptable face of the unacceptable facts of reality. I've made mistakes, of course; I can admit that and I have to really because everyone knows I have. I could blame others, and did frequently, but sole responsibility comes with leadership and in the end that wretched buck stops in your headlights, no matter how you try and spin it.

I can't remember when reality took fake over fact. We had so many intelligent people looking into it, people with letters after their names who had dedicated their lives to the imminent destruction of the world, this merry chorus of doom and despair that they were, you'd think they would at least know how to sing from the same song sheet, wouldn't you? The truth, as unpalatable as it may be, was that they were; it just got sullied in communication and communication wrung every last drop of truth from it until reality became fiction. Until it became what sells, became what people demand. You know, it's strange, but I think some people wanted it to be true, the press, the television, the Internet; they took a rumour and made a story, fuelled a fear and turned the screw so tight that even the perpetuators of the myth were beginning to doubt their own embellishments. The country changed overnight and people went nuts. I should have gone to the people and told them that it wasn't true before now. I should have done the right thing and I was going to, I really was – I mean, there are some things you can't get away with and proclaiming the end of the world does kind of box you into a corner – but I tell you, a lie can carry a lot of power and temptation. I could go back on TV and tell them I was wrong and apologise, but I doubt people are even watching anymore. Real life has finally become more interesting.

I'm not prone to looking back and indulging my regrets, but somehow it seems too hard not to these days. It seems to make sense. I'd like to have travelled more, certainly, that's a big regret. Properly travelled, I mean; taken in the sights and lived a time in other places. Albie and I were going to run away together – well, I say that, I hadn't actually asked her; I just like to imagine she'd say yes. But then, with Albie, destination would have been difficult; she's very picky. She would never have gone anywhere hot, she doesn't like the sun. "Shit looks the same in the sun," she said to me once. She'd have liked to go to Scandinavia. Alaska. Somewhere like that. Taken a boat as close to one of the poles as she could – she's a cold person, is Albie. She always wanted to go and see the Northern Lights as well; that was her ideal holiday, she said. She had asked Zach to take her there once but he told her that he thought Blackpool was rubbish. She didn't ask again. I was going to take her, I had made plans, I was just going to bundle her onto a plane and surprise her. I didn't, though. Somewhere between the idea and the desire, life got in the way.

I'd liked to have had sex on the beach as well. Ever since I saw "From Here To Eternity", frolicking on a beach with a beautiful woman while the waves came crashing in always struck me as a romantic idea. I'm not averse to romantic notions, even now. Never done that, though; the closest I ever got was when my PA gave me crabs my first year in office. Good old Estelle, who would ever have known she would climb so high on the ladder so very fast? She was ever so good to me. As soon as I took office I asked her to get me a red phone and she did. I said I wanted a red phone on my office desk; I wanted it connected to someone important, I said. Sometimes, when I was in a meeting with a particularly irritating bastard who was trying to get something from me, I would casually stroke the receiver whilst talking. It was important for them to know who had the power in the room. I had a red phone, ergo I was the most important person in the room. I'm still thinking and talking like any of it means anything any more. It's just small words of no real importance. We are all as irrelevant as each other now. Geniuses and fools break just as easily.

I can't believe it's been less than a fortnight since I gave that speech, and already the cracks are starting to show. Schuttler and Wise are good enough to publish the crime figures every day and it really is shocking. I searched out the statistics for my old neighbourhood and in three days the crime rate had gone up 70 percent. There had been two murders in my old street alone. It was shocking, not least because one of them hadn't been that old bastard at number 52 who used to flash at people from his kitchen window.

I didn't question at the time why the lawyers came in so quickly. Albie had said that they were always there, anyway, running the show from the shadows, waiting for that perfect moment to strike like a vengeful spurned lover. As soon as the report came in and the Chinese whispers spread amongst the corridors of parliament they were there, ready, waiting for me to fuck up. They didn't have to wait long. Perhaps it was always this way. I do feel like I had power; I know that some of the decisions were mine. I did sign a lot of papers and forms without reading them but I was always told what they were and they sounded fine to me. I left a lot of it up to Albie as my chief advisor. Sure, she couldn't advise piss up a wall, but she had star wattage and that goes a long way. She was the only choice for that role, really, but I had to persuade her to take the job. It's never easy with Albie; there was a lot of wining and dining, which I suppose in hindsight was actually foreplay masquerading as a job offer, though let it be said from me that at the time it was just the job. I had no intention of having sex with her. I'm sure the same could be said for her as she left the first meal by calling me a "shallow venomous little twat."

Albie and I spoke the day of the speech. She had phoned to tell me about Zach, to let me know that she was out of here, gone, long gone and soon forgotten. I begged her to make the speech instead of me, I wanted one last chance to be with her, one more moment in a fake sun. I tried to tell her that she always came across better on TV than me – because let's be honest, we all know she did – but even that little tickle to her vanity wasn't enough. She knew that this was a gig where someone was going to die on their arse. Fair enough, I suppose; her's is an arse worth saving. "The public elected you," she said to me as some sort of justification. If only that were true. It wasn't me they elected; we just got them to close their eyes and count to ten. We haven't spoken since then. I went and hid in a bottle, drank away the hours, snorted this, chewed on that, and by the time the speech came around I was wrecked. In hindsight I probably should have sobered up first but, well, have we not all made mistakes? Was I not the biggest of all those mistakes? You're thinking it so you might as well say it.

I was. You make a mistake and you might break something; a teacup maybe or at worst a heart. I made a mistake and I broke a country. All things being equal, you don't even come a close second.

She was always great with people, was Albie; she had the common touch, by which I mean she made common people feel special, which I suppose is what TV is all about now. People trusted her and liked her. I certainly did. That first day on 'So You Want To Be Prime Minister?' was really nerve-wracking. I was just a plumber, what did I know about TV? But she was there, cup of tea and a cuddle for all the contestants, a big smile and kind words, telling us which camera to work, which side of our faces would look better. We worked on witty little anecdotes together; she told us that we would all be expected to regale the public with little stories about ourselves, some humorous little interlude, and I was struggling. I just couldn't think of anything remotely interesting or funny but we got together and talked it through. She helped me with it and eventually we settled for a story about my tie catching fire from a Flaming Sambuca in a cocktail bar whilst I was on my stag do. She said people would like that and that even if they didn't it didn't really matter as they could make it sound like they did. It's amazing to think of what we became and what we did, but every story must have a beginning, I suppose, no matter how insignificant, and ours began trying to concoct a pithy aside from my bullshit life. It's been an odd few years.

The day after the speech, I woke up hung-over in an old hotel. The room was trashed and I had no idea whether it had been me or someone else. The video of my speech was playing on a TV in front of me, playing loud and through big garish colours, like the biggest pissed regret you could ever have, hanging on the edges of your subconscious mind like wet laundry. I was stripped to my pants and there was cocaine powder littered around my navel. I could hear talking outside the hotel door, low whispers and just the occasional laugh. My head felt like a warm boiled egg and I gently cupped it in my hand as I sat and surveyed the room once again, looking for a memory.

I had been in the room before, I remembered that much. I had been there with Albie. At that memory, a small knot pinged loose in my stomach and Zach's face loomed over me like guilt come alive. His bird-like face on squat shoulders above his pigeon chest, painted onto the insides of my eyes, and around the room in every spare inch of wall. I've known guilt before. In fact, I've grown so accustomed to the sensation that I struggle to feel it anymore. I hate Zach and I'm jealous of him, it may not be justification enough for what I intend to do but it's what I have. It makes sense to me and, quite frankly, your opinion doesn't matter. You can still hate someone you love, it's quite a stupid thing but no less true for it. I do love Zach, always will I suppose, but I can't stop hating him either, and in the end, that is the emotion that brings the action because it's easier. Not that I regret what happened; I certainly don't regret Albie and I, quite the opposite. I love her to a wreck. I just regret the hold Zach has always had over her. You can never regret love unless you never have it. Then it's not so much regretting love but your own worthless life.

I was about to try and stand when I could hear a tap running in the en-suite bathroom and spun around with a start; water was splashing in a sink and a tune was being whistled, a tune I couldn't remember, the sort of irritating tune that signals the arrival of an ice cream van or a milkman. I was still sat, ogling the bathroom door and trying to place the tune when Edgerton walked into the room, wiping blood from his hands and wrists on a towel and offering forth the sort of beaming smile that could make a hung-over man murder. He's always been an optimist, has Edgerton, always a smile and a cheery disposition, always hated by most. I liked him when I first met him; he had been charming and enigmatic, had won my wife and I over instantly. We had been holidaying by the sea. I forget the place, some ghastly little old England wet dream that still clings on like a kiss-me-quick hat on the head of a slag to its status of worth. He had been there reading palms at the seafront and my wife had bought into that notion immediately; we had been married less than a year and already we knew we had made a mistake. I think she had gone to him for answers, she liked all that business; she had said that she wanted reassurance but I knew all she really wanted from him was a way out. An excuse. I suppose she maybe wanted him to tell her that she was to meet a tall dark stranger and she could then legitimately fuck the first that staggered by and call it an act of fate. Like I could talk. I had already had a bunk-up with the owner of our B&B in a laundry cupboard. My infidelity has always been my old faithful; it never disappoints or deserts.

He had given us both a reading and had said nothing much to either of us until we made to leave. At that point, he grabbed me back and made me sit again, staring deep into my face as if seeing it for the first time. He seemed to be convulsing and gyrating, seat boogying to his own tune. My wife thought he was having a fit and ran out screaming. Edgerton gripped me tight, pulled me to him and breathed words to me that then, and even more so now, make my balls tighten, and not always in a good way. "You will be the change we need Archie, and the change we fear," was what he said to me. "The stranger will come and your time will be born. Fear nothing but the limits of your imagination." With that, Edgerton slumped forward and started sleeping. I had stayed for a minute, watching him, checking his pulse to make sure he hadn't expired, and then left to rejoin my wife. He had squatted himself into my life at that point, and when his prophecy bore out he was clearly the logical choice when I decided to hire a spiritual advisor. I kept it secret, of course. The tabloids may think nothing of helping elevate a plumber to the biggest seat in the land but they would have had a field day if they thought for a moment that I had any beliefs.

'You're awake, Archie?' Edgerton asked in a statement, tossing the towel away and sitting on the edge of the bed.

'With such extraordinary perception, I wonder why you never were a gambling man, Edgerton dear fellow. You could make the money to rule the world.'

'It doesn't take money, Archie; it takes imagination and it takes heart.'

'Bollocks.'

'I suppose it also takes bollocks too.' Edgerton nodded to the TV and the disgraced has-been trussed up in a badly fitting suit that was speaking into the screen. 'Quite the show you put on last night. You've scared a lot people.'

'It was a mistake.'

'Yes, it was, but people don't know that.'

'Don't be ridiculous, someone will tell them. The newspapers will kick my arse around town for a bit, tell them it's all fine, and tomorrow they can go back to star-fucking and immigrant baiting. The end of the world is tomorrow's chip paper. Or something. Fuck them.'

It was at that point that Edgerton leaned down, picked up a pile of newspapers from by the door to the room and flung them onto the bed. He said nothing, nor did he need to; the horror was all there to see on the front pages. Headlines shrieked back at me in the biggest, boldest type, wailing in my face, and for the first time the full realisation of what I had started fingered my spine and jabbed my shit-faced head with the force of a bullet. "THE BEGINNING OF THE END", said one quite cryptically; "THE DAY THE COUNTRY DIED", ran another. "WE'RE DOOMED", said the tattiest tit tripe on the shelves. "FOUR HORSEMEN ENTER COUNTRY ILLEGALLY", said another, but my favourite was "BUTCHER HEADLINES END-OF-THE-WORLD TV SHOW", and that made me laugh heartily despite Edgerton's stern face. I imagined there was already a group of men in thick rimmed glasses and pastel coloured shirts, workshopping the end-of-the-world show in a windowless room congested with the stench of coffee breath and desperation. It had to be true. Imagine the ratings.

'I don't understand it.'

'You don't understand what sells, you mean? Surely you do, Archie.'

'But they know it's not true…'

'The press? You want to think about that for a minute?'

'Yes, of course, but…'

'There is the truth and there is the story. The truth will come out of course, but it may be too late.'

'What do I do? We can blame Zach's kid, right?

Dippy, ducky do-right? Right? It was all his fault anyway, we can blame him. That gets me out of it, right?'

I should explain about Zach's son. Maybe Zach too; both have been pretty much a big part of my story. I grew close to Zach when Albie came on board. You could sense there was a lot of bitterness between them still; Albie had said it was because her solo career had taken off with the show and Zach found that a little hard to take, but personally I don't think it was that involved. I think they simply had moved out of love and into politeness and routine. At least I know Albie had. I like to think that were they still happy I would never have got together with Albie. I've done wrong with so many right women but I've never betrayed a friend before. Wife, yes, of course; friend, not before now. It feels weird. I got Zach on board as my troubleshooter, my right hand; he dealt with the media mostly, he knew that world and he knew how to play it, how to charm with a velvet tongue in a steel jaw. His unhinged being made him a natural. We decided, as soon as we got in, that we had to make a deal with the press, with the media; they had funnelled us into power and we all knew how quickly they could break us. Albie said as much at the start. "The media are the real rulers," and she was right. Looking at me I was just their bastard son, and it was time to start shaking the hand that fed.

I suppose it was a coalition of sorts. We would work together. They would be your bridge, your conduit, and the fervent supporter of your viewpoints and, in return, the hacks and the hounds would have 24-hour access to me and it would all be shown on the TV and written about in the papers. You would have, if not a voice, at least a front-row view. It was a modern democracy in a new bloom. One hand washes the other and we were all going to be adult about it, we were in it together, after all, so being adult seemed the best way to progress. I promised so many things back then, we all did; I promised there would be honesty, I promised accessibility and, more than anything, I promised that there would be transparency. I knew, with the media behind us, no one would ever see through me. Sweep up the ignorant and the blank and bombard them with what they want to hear. It's what TV does best and nowadays it's the only way to work this show. I suppose that if I'm honest, I was always subconsciously waiting for them to turn and bite. It was a fickle inevitability. Here they were then; finally biting.

Zach would have been better at the speech than me, almost anyone would I guess, but Zach was a raving lunatic and had just found out that I had been having an affair with his wife. I didn't think it the better of best ideas to ask him, but he really could bring even the most moribund material to life. I suppose years in kids' TV make you a master at sugar-coating shit. He could have done it well. But, well, he was mad. I had been expecting him to come barging in to see me once he'd found out about Albie and I, to phone me up screaming some sort of retribution, some vengeance, but there was nothing. No word, no threat, no promise, and that in its quiet self was all the more frightening. I know I will have to face what I've done at some point, and I know that I will have to try out being a man about it. I'm just fighting for time at the moment, I suppose. Time has stopped meaning much, yet grows more vital by the day.

All this started with Zach's son, the "environmental renegade" as he liked to be called, the "cock" as he was called, that pungently scented sandal-wearing love-muncher. He was this government's bête noire from the start; the fantasy living do-gooder. I should have put my carbon footprint up his backside on day dot and got him in line, but I gave him too much rope. Of course here's a bastard who didn't have the good grace to hang himself with it but to simply ask if it was biodegradable. Zach introduced me to him, the cock in hemp, and asked me to employ him. I got him to head up the office for the environment, you know, trees and rivers and that thing with the ice caps. The whole green thing was becoming Middle England's "get-into-heaven-free card" so I had to make an effort. He seemed to understand what everyone was getting into a twist about so I just let him get on with it. That I suppose was another mistake to chalk up, maybe the biggest; I gave a man with ideas and opinions power. I never thought I'd be a political radical.

Anyone with a rational mind would know it was a lie. So why should we be in this situation? Why would I need to apologise? There are, I'm sure, still sensible minds out there that know that it isn't the end of the world. There must be a man with a beard somewhere who could tell people the truth. Anyway, what would I say to the public in such a situation? "Sorry, but it turns out that you aren't all going to die in Mother Nature's shit storm but merely have a rather soggy autumn?" Of course, as soon as he sold me the lie, that long-haired, sandal-sucking, don't-wear-underwear, peace-loving cock wrangler disappeared to the nearest jungle and bedded in, glad-handing lepers and recycling his piss. Never trust a man with ideals. What was I thinking? I'm not taking the blame for this. I didn't concoct this story. He should be standing in front of the country and apologising! He's the one who rigged the numbers and tarted up the facts. The country could be wiped out in forty-four minutes, he claimed! Under-funded, he said. He couldn't save the country on the budget we afforded him. The arrogance! I gave his reports to Albie and told her to cut through the trees and let me see the forest. He really let his imagination loose on that dossier; it was the first time, the only time, that I heard Albie cry. She was terrified, hysterical, screaming of a life unlived and things she never had done. She started to kiss me, tore at my clothes and forced herself on me.

It was the moment I knew it was love. Impending Armageddon had forced honesty from our lips and it tasted good. People cleverer than I knew that the report wasn't worth the paper it was printed on or the tree that was felled for its lie, but there is power in the lie, and besides, was integrity ever really expected from me? I know, I'm a terrible man, so what? Sue me. I can give you the number of some good lawyers.

'I've just had a religious experience in your bathroom.' It was, it's fair to say, not what I was expecting Edgerton to say, now or at even the most surreal future, but there you go, he'd put it out there and was looking at me with a smile, waiting for me to care.

'Yes, I think I must have had one in there last night myself.'

'It's the most wonderful thing. He came to me with a glorious gift.'

'I'm apoplectic with joy.'

'You don't understand.'

'No, not so much.'

'He came to me.'

'Who?'

'The man. The main man.'

'I thought I was the main man.'

'THE man.'

'Who's that?'

'He's calling himself John this time around.'

'John?'

'John.'

'Lawyer?'

'Listen…'

'Have you seen my clothes?'

'Archie, listen, you must listen, I have great things to tell you, advice to offer – is it not what you pay me for, to advise you?'

'I'm not paying you anything any more, dear fellow. Didn't you smell the waft of Old Spice amongst the corridors of power? There's a new sheriff in town and he wears the best suits. Our salad days are long gone; we're onto the coffee and cigars now.' I looked at him for a moment, waiting for him to relent. This is what always used to happen when it was clear I had finished a conversation – people shut up and pissed off – but Edgerton was starting to hop from side to side and carry the sort of smug look that makes you want to peel someone's face off and slap them with it.

'You're not a religious man, are you, Archie?'

'Not so much, dear fellow; that's a mythology even TV can't sell.'

'You are blinkered, perhaps? Closed off?'

'I'm an open book. A pop-up book perhaps, but still an open book.'

'You are a spiritual man, I think; it's that spiritual connection that brought you to me many years ago. It is the tie that binds us still.'

'Not so much, Edgerton. I thought you could tell the future.'

'Would that were so.'

'Indeed. Yeah, good point, you're obviously shit, you're fired.'

'I don't need a job any more, I have a calling.'

'How nice for you. Couldn't call up a cup of coffee and an elephant bollock-sized aspirin, could you?'

Edgerton reached into his jacket and pulled out the sort of shiny envelope that usually fits in at award ceremonies and could only contain something of the utmost unimportance. He began waving it around in the air in front of me, playfully jabbing it towards me like he were trying to fence with it. I merely sat and stared, unsure how to proceed with a man who had clearly lost the plot. Perhaps if I had tried then, at that seemingly insignificant moment with my spiritual advisor, I might now be better equipped to deal with circumstances now that so many have followed suit. I shuffled forward on the bed and swung my legs to the floor, the soft impact sending jagged spears up through my hips and through my fragile body, into my egg-like head, cracking it open from the inside. I swore words that I hadn't sworn before and stood in a stagger, falling immediately into a chair by the bed.

'You must listen to me.'

'Not if you shut the fuck up I don't.'

'There is going to be a knock on the door in a

minute. It will be Punkley and he will try and encourage you to join him outside for a meeting. There will be lawyers there and they will try and lead you away. They want to destroy you, Archie. They will destroy you. You must not go with them.'

'Why not?'

'Because I can save you. This envelope can save you.'

'Sharp enough for a papercut to the throat, is it?'

'Don't be defeatist.'

Punkley is a complete bastard, a wiry wide boy with drowned eyes and a face that looks like it has been mined. He's my Home Secretary and a former career criminal. He's done a lot of TV and adverts and things, quite an in-demand voiceover artist he was, but you probably knew that anyway. Zach met him on the video shoot for Mr. Chuff's first single, "Doing the Chuff." Punkley was playing Mr. Chuff. I'm sure you know the video I mean; it was that one with the life-sized Mr. Chuff frolicking on the beach with that big-titted bit from that soap opera? Sure you do. You probably bought the CD, you sad pathetic wretch. Anyway, Punkley and Zach bonded during a drinking session in one of the capital's less salubrious drinking dens after getting into a fight and beating a pimp to a pulp. He wasn't necessarily the obvious choice for Home Secretary, but Zach was certainly enthused and I suppose I probably didn't care as much back then as I do now that it matters. Punkley always wanted my job. It was clear from the start; you could tell from the looks and the threats. But it could never have happened, not with his colourful past.

There was a knock on the door, swiftly followed by Punkley's unmistakable growl scratching at the wood, huffing and puffing and threatening to blow us all down. Edgerton looked at me with a disgustingly triumphant smirk and for a second even put his hands on his hips like the worst sort of superhero. I just sat in my chair, looking through Edgerton to the door, realising that I couldn't stand and hoping that he wouldn't talk to me for too long. Edgerton pocketed the envelope and patted his jacket before turning to the door, yanking it open and ushering Punkley in with a dramatic flourish.

'What you doing here, you gnarling clotpole?' Punkley said to Edgerton and pushed past him, scuttling into the room in small, narrow, darting steps, a rifle slung over one shoulder and a small cigar poking from one corner of his mouth. Somehow I didn't think to question the rifle. Somehow it seemed to fit. I guess that was the moment it started – for me, anyway. I don't care how it started for you.

Punkley took a seat on a small table and gently rested the rifle from the window, staring back through the telescopic sight down at the street below. 'One hell of a storm you created, Archie, no pun intended. It must be true what they used to say, "television adds ten pounds to the lie." Look at them all down there.'

'I can't stand. Why don't you describe it to me in your own inimitable lurid fashion, dear Mr. Punkley?'

'Fuckers running riot.'

'Why were you never my speech writer?'

'Haven't you seen the news?'

'Of course not. I never watch the news. It's just repeats to me. I am the news.'

'Not anymore, dick itch.'

'Explain?'

'Look at them!'

I looked to Edgerton, that revolting self-satisfied grin still stretching his face flat and I shrugged; Edgerton just patted his pocket again to signify something that was clearly lost on me. I sighed heavily and farted, standing with the ease of a post-fuck pensioner and staggered to the window, unable to even care about my balls which I knew were poking from the bottom of my pants. Staring down at the street below, it wasn't immediately identifiable what had got Punkley so excited, but slowly, as I stood there staring through my reflection, warped with a sheet of condensation, I started to see it. There were people running back and forth across the street, running into shops and back out again with goods. The electrical hardware shop opposite was bearing the brunt; TVs were being stolen, cameras, phones – even a polystyrene mannequin with a pair of headphones on his head was carted out. Between these people, a man – one would assume the proprietor –

was hitting as many of the people as he could with a metal pole. Next door, a small food store was being raided by a group of people. They carted food out along a human chain whilst a rotund man rolled on the pavement in a pool of blood, his little legs kicking the air like he was trying to turn himself over. Further along, people were fighting in clusters of concentrated aggression like wasps on a picnic spread. Some would break off and attach themselves to another group; others just stood their ground, punching and kicking, hair pulling and biting. Two cars shot past, bumper to bumper, swerving across the road and mounting the pavements, colliding with shop fronts and other cars. Another car screeched to a halt next to one group of fighters and the driver stepped out and jumped into the huddle, disappearing in a blur of swinging arms and kicking legs until he was no longer identifiable. His car was set on within a few seconds; a group of children appearing seemingly from nowhere and destroying it with cricket bats and bricks.

I watched it all happen, yet it felt like I was a million miles away, as if I were merely watching TV and all that played out was scripted action from willing players. I realise now that it actually was. At that moment, though, I simply turned back to the room and gently slipped my balls back into my pants.

'I could shoot someone right now and it wouldn't matter,' Punkley said into the air, almost as if he were testing the temperature of opinion. 'What you did in your speech is take away consequence. What actually matters, at the end of the world? You can fucking do anything!'

'Yes, now I might have been a bit mistaken by that.'

'Of course you were, but what does that matter? It's in the papers, on the news – people believe it. People want to believe it. People can do just whatever they damn well want! You know who I keep thinking about? That wanker at school that stole Sally Bergan off me. You know what I'm gonna do? I'm going to search him out and cut off his dick.'

'Steady on, old man. We may be set fair for a couple of crazy days but this will all settle down. There will still be order. You just can't simply kill anyone, you know?'

'Says the Prime Minister. Who are we at war with at the moment? I forget.'

'Yes, me too. But that's no excuse.'

'You think this is going to stop? How foolish are you really, Archie? Every action has a consequence…'

'Exactly…'

'An eye for an eye, a tooth for a tooth… One murder means at least one more guaranteed. Don't you see how this is going to blossom?'

'In the kingdom of the blind, the one-eyed man is king.'

'Yeah, and in a toothless country being blind is probably a blessing.'

I could see Punkley straining at the trigger. His eyes were narrowed so much they looked like knife slits in plasticine. A horrid rattling growl was gathering in his throat as he fixated on, then turned away from, some unseen sight, some faceless person down below on the street. He pulled the rifle back and slowly rested it against his arm, breathing slowly, the growl fading into a stutter as he turned his watering eye slits on me with a disdain he clearly felt he no longer had to hide 'You're wanted, Prime Minister.'

'Is that so?' I looked back to the hotel room door and saw two well-dressed men standing either side of the frame, their ghostly blank faces waiting to fit whatever situation arose. I knew from the well-manicured fingers and eye bleeding aftershave that they were lawyers, and I knew without even looking at Edgerton that his grin was still there. 'And may I get dressed first?'

'You look a fucking mess,' was Punkley's response to my request, an affirmative hiding as an insult, which is the way, in my experience, that most little men like to conduct their business. Punkley withdrew, pulling the doors to with a gentle click and I looked to Edgerton and then immediately looked away again, my hangover firming to lead around my brain and pressing me down in to the carpet. I looked around the room for my clothes but saw nothing everywhere, except one lonely sock hanging from the light shade. I had clearly had a wonderful evening – no doubt my last in some time –

and I was so utterly furious that I couldn't remember any of it.

'They are going to hang you out to dry, Archie. You do know that, don't you?'

'Maybe that's what needs to happen.'

'You will have to answer for what you did.'

'I know. Where are my clothes? Are they in the bathroom?' They weren't. I roamed the room, retrieved the one sock and dusted my navel down and gummed my fingers clean of the cocaine. 'Where are my clothes?'

'I need you to spread his word to your people.'

'What?'

'He told me I had to entrust this envelope to you…'

'Me?'

'Someone who people will listen to. I think he feels a bit self-conscious; I think he believes that people wouldn't listen to him if he spoke. You've been on the telly, you're famous – people will hang off your every word. Has not yesterday born that out, Archie? You can do anything.'

'I can't find my fucking clothes!'

'He chose me as his vessel, I choose you as his messenger to the world. Do you not see what a glorious honour this is, Archie? You have been touched by the most wondrous love.'

'You really are a twat, aren't you?'

'What I have could change the world.'

'Fuck it, you get tired of all that shit after a while. I wish I was still a plumber.' I really did. At that point, the memories of my happy years at Laker & Butcher Plumbing Services were an hourly occurrence. That whole week I would often find my hand over the phone, fingers itching to make the call to old man Laker, just to see how things were, see if he needed a hand or two. Life, as in love, can often not be valued until you make a complete balls-up of it all.

'You don't want to change the world?'

'I'm slightly more interested in changing into some clothes. Besides, no one ever changed the world in his pants. What is it, anyway?'

'A glorious thing.'

'Yes, you said. Don't be cryptic, Edgerton, you aren't able to hold people's interest long enough to pull it off.'

'It is a gift to the world. An offering, a direction, the first step towards a functioning world, free from confusion and a lack of imagination. We live in a world where we never look to improve or progress; we have stalled in our own image, simply recycling all our old evils and failings, offering them as tired management to forlorn and submissive people. This can change all that and we can step into a new dawn with courage and optimism.'

'Oh my, you are a tedious man, aren't you?'

'It is the last original idea in the world.'

'Excuse me?'

'I think you heard.'

Edgerton tiptoed to the bedroom door and gently

wedged a chair against the door handles. 'This is the most important thing. Not your apologies and your contrition. We both know that will do no good. Schuttler & Wise need a fall guy, they need a patsy – they need you to die for them, Archie. But if you take this, if you take the last original idea in the world to your people, you can stop this country falling into chaos. Your people can rise again and you can be reborn and you can hold onto your power. You can – and I use this term sparingly, believe me – be a god, Archie. You can change the world.'

At Edgerton's words, there was a kick to the bedroom door and the chair began to strain as the lawyers tried to get back into the room. I needed time to think, I needed my clothes and I needed another drink. But I suppose when you are asked to be a god, such things have to come secondary to your responsibilities. As the door began to splinter, as fists rained down on the wood and the hinges began to sigh, I just looked at Edgerton and nodded.

'People will kill for this, Archie. Do you understand that?'

'Who?' It was a stupid question, of course, but I believe that the situation allowed me a few of them.

Edgerton looked back at the door and then back at me as he took the envelope out and held it in front of him. 'Those who crave power.'

I looked at the envelope and then down at my

nakedness, my dignity held by one sock and pants that hoped to see better days again. 'I don't really have anywhere to put it, old chap, perhaps you would be so good as to hold on to it for me? And forgive me asking the obvious, for it seems we have moved beyond that planet, but how do we get out of here?'

As a lawyer's beautiful hand broke through the wood of the door and groped for Edgerton, my spiritual advisor and apparent lunatic, merely pointed at the window with a finger. The blood at his hands and wrists now, it would seem, not there anymore or perhaps faded out of reality like a superimposed image of a drunken dream. Edgerton walked forward briskly and led me to the window, opening it and staring down.

'We can climb down to the next balcony. From there we can jump.'

'I'm in my pants!'

'Don't worry, Archie, you're the Prime Minister; I think your modesty is the least of your concerns. Tuck your genitals in first though, there may be children down there.'

Politicians don't sell black and white anymore. It's a roaring trade in grey. I learned that as soon as I took office. You are handed civil servants like hors d'œuvres and you just kind of let them get on with it. Sure, you throw a few ideas into the pot, but in the end you are just a face for a dartboard. The whole business of politics is so confusing to me now, more confusing than it ever was and I was never a political animal. Each scandal, each let-down and each ineffectual little man that stepped into the suit neutered me till I just couldn't get it up to care anymore. I voted twice. Never really had a party, never really cared. If I'm being honest, when I applied to go on the show, I didn't even know what it was for. A friend of mine, a fairly proficient spoon player who was always trying out for talent shows, wanted to go on it so I tagged along and thought I'd give it a go. I do a pretty mean Bing Crosby turn – it was always my party piece – so I got that out and dusted it down; that got me through to the next round and we were off. At the time, I didn't really want to be Prime Minister, but the pay was better than I had ever had, and, as my friend said, the travel perks would be quite fun. So what the heck, I thought I'd give it a go.

When I started I was schooled in political correctness, as apparently there are certain things you can't say as Prime Minister. Who knew? It's so confusing now. There were so many things to remember that I can't actually remember what we are supposed to be anymore. They call ticket inspectors ambassadors now. Did you know that? Ambassadors for what? The marginalised in society? I can't remember what nationalities we are allowed to like anymore, I simply can't. I keep thinking back to what Punkley said to me. "Who are we at war with at the moment?" I really don't know anymore. Someone does though, I'm sure, so don't worry; though I suppose that's irrelevant now anyway. Our next war is going to be a little closer to home. I doubt we will forget anymore.

Now the lawyers are crawling out of the cracks, the whole thing is even more confusing. I should have listened to Albie, she knew and always said that they would be the first at the door, sucking life from the last few places that has it. I should have bombed the lot of them, I could probably have done that, I had a red phone. "A fool with the keys to too many locks," Albie once said. Well, it doesn't matter any more. Perhaps we should all jump in a bottle deep enough and we can all sleep through until this madness passes. I wish I could feel the liberation of having faith in people, I really do, but I can't. I've built a career from people's stupidity and their response of lunacy and anarchy simply justifies my lack of faith. Maybe it should all have been true; maybe that would have been the answer. I struggle to find anyone worth saving, anyway. We were going to do great things. We really were, Albie and I, me and my dear friend Zach; we all meant the best for the country no matter the sham of our rule. But I suppose, in the end, we just simply perpetuated the myth of importance. Perhaps that's the secret, maybe that's the job description. It isn't about effecting change, merely sustaining the illusion.

I can't stop thinking about Zach. I should feel guiltier

than I do, I know I should; an ounce of humanity would do it. Anything. But I find it hard. I think that's why I think of him so often, because I'm fearful of what I have become. I knew I would have to shed some level of decency in taking the job, and I did; the rest fell away when I fell in love. You don't get rules in love. There is no book. There is no guide worth a jot. It's something you just have to make up as you go along, and make it up I did. Whatever thread it is that unravels in your mind and ties you to someone, it is a force not to be messed with. If we could bottle that, we could solve anything, cure all, and destroy everything. Maybe that is the last original idea left in the world. I would like to think it was that.

Of course it's questionable, in regards to Zach, that a madman should have been allowed so close to the keys to the country, but I maintain we have had worse higher up the ladder. He was just a little destroyed. It was nothing a little bit of responsibility wouldn't sort out; a goal and a purpose can do wonders for a person. That's what Albie and I decided. Zach's personality disorder was a closely guarded secret, of course; I mean, he was a personality, so naturally any sort of malfunction wouldn't have been good for the career and you know, by and large he kept it all in check. That was of course mainly down to Albie. She was great for him. Not so great the other way round, of course, because she was never going to be a martyr to a man forever. The fact that it was I who talked Albie into staying with him kills me daily by doses; it's death by a thousand question marks. I have gone through that decision in my mind so often and have yet to really deliver satisfactory answers. I think in the end it came down simply to trying to safeguard Zach's state of mind. We were both a bit worried what he might do without her, or rather I was worried what he would do to me if he found out. I knew that Albie didn't have the heart to carry that burden far. If either of us had bothered to look at what we were taking from her, that she would leave us both in the end was probably a given. Neither of us deserved her. I had hoped that once Schuttler & Wise shipped them both out I could wallow in the old safeguard of "out of sight, out of mind", but this was not the case. You can numb pain when you don't see the affliction, but the sickness remains. Albie always used to make me feel sick; that was how I knew it was love. Nothing on this earth, no victory, no creation, no human greatness can compete with love. I think when Albie and I shared our last kiss, that was probably the time I first realised that I would have to kill Zach.

Edgerton nimbly jumped on to the balcony railing below the room, swung back, grabbed the railing and let himself fall onto a grass verge at the front of the hotel, looking up at me and patting his hands together like a parent encouraging their child's first steps. I straddled the window ledge and tried to lift myself over, teetering there for a few minutes, wobbling and convinced that I was just going to dive down headfirst. In the end, it was the final shattering of the door and the two lawyers descending towards me with all their magnificently clean fury that got me moving. I swung my other leg over and fell, the metal bar of the below balcony rising up and nestling perfectly and heavily between my legs with a dull clanking sound, a sound starting a sensation that I still find myself recalling from time to time, even now.

There are, I'm sure, many painful sensations in this world. I remember a story of a club owner I met many years ago with unfeasibly large balls who once sat on them, and I remember him telling me how he had to dangle them in a bucket of ice for a week, of course I'm sure a lot of women will tell you that childbirth can be a very painful experience, and who am I to say any different? But when all the cards are counted and the chips divvied up I would venture that unless you gave birth to a two-ton circus freak baby that came out of you sideways strapped to a gurney, then I don't believe anyone can appreciate the level of pain involved at that precise moment. I fell forward, thudded my forehead against the pole and then fell like a rag to the grass below, my eyes watering and my teeth seemingly growing out of my gums and threatening to chew my chin off. I was vaguely aware of gunshots but was totally uninterested, indeed even when Edgerton told me later that they started shooting at us as we hightailed it across to the hotel car park I still couldn't bring myself to care. A man and his balls have a relationship that very few can compete with, particularly when they are the size of cantaloupes.

I must have slept or blocked out most of what happened next. I can only remember staring up at the roof of a car as I gently tried to massage my balls back to normality, breathing in the cheap leather upholstery and trying to stop myself shivering. Edgerton told me later that we were chased, that the smashed window and bullet holes were the result of gunfire from our pursuers, but I only mumbled and nodded, caring only to be dressed and elsewhere. I shifted up slightly on the back seat, meaning to look from the side window and try and pinpoint our location by a building or a house, something from the images that were zipping past at a blurred impossible speed, but as I did I found my attention being diverted by the car radio. It was a voice I recognised, words that were familiar, all playing louder than either deserved, and then, slowly, it all fell into place. It was me. It was my speech. Every word formed a kick at my naked body; every rise and fall of my dreadfully drunk voice was the crack of a whip at my ears.

'Turn that damn thing off!' I yelled at the back of Edgerton's head, surprising him and making him swerve across lanes.

'I can't! Damn it, Archie, don't shout at me when I'm driving.'

'What do you mean, you can't? Twiddle the knob, second nature to a first-class wanker, surely?'

'They shot the stereo up. The thing is stuck. I can't, look…' I did, and he was right; the stereo was broken and hanging off its base, knobless and pathetic. 'I'm sorry Archie, nothing I can do about it.'

I slumped on to the back seat and closed my arms around my face. My words floated around me, coming in like little daggers, and I curled my body up tight on the smooth leather seats, desperately waiting for it to stop or for something else to start.

I think I'm a trifle pissed. Me. Yeah! Your leader. Your figurehead. Look at my face! Look at my beautiful face! Fucking people. So here we are, just you and me, back where we started, me on the telly and you watching and listening to everything I say cos I'm important and you're not. Okay? Actually, I wonder just how many of you are watching right now. I've checked the schedules, there's tits on the other side, yeah, proper big tits and they are European tits too so you might get a bit more if you stick with it, and there's also a quiz show where you can phone up and change your life, and there's a documentary about some freak born with a dick on his shoulder. True. Flick over now and have a look. I will wait.

You still here? Bet you aren't. I'm supposed to stand here and talk to you about the imminent destruction of the country. I have to. I don't want to. I have nothing to say to you wretched bunch of wankers. You've probably heard the rumours, that Mother Nature is pissed. I'm pissed. I know that I can do pretty much anything when pissed. I'm supposed to put your minds at rest. Yeah. That. I'm supposed to do that. But I'm not going to. No. Bollocks to you. Not one of you worth saving anyway. Well, no, there is one. But she's fucked off. So why should I care anymore? I don't. It should have been Albie stood here talking to you. She cares more about people than I do. Ssshh! I didn't say that. Well I did. My beloved Albie. We've been... y'know... been... What's the best way of saying this... erm... we've been... Albie and I... Oh bollocks, what do you care? It can't go anywhere, she's left, she's gone, and she's flown away. You're not even listening to me, are you?

There was a time when Prime Ministers spoke that the country held on their every word. There was a time when the job and the incum... incu... cucumbent were respected. Where's the love? Why don't you love me anymore? Because the country's gonna end? Because the storms are gonna make the rivers rise, and the hail is going to come down like boulders and the fires are going to tear this place flat? Well that's no fucking excuse, is it? It's all I want, you know? To be loved... Is that asking too much? You should turn to those you love in such times as this. But not you lot, right? Hearts of stone you lot, let's just see what you do at the end... I know what I'm going to do, I'm going to get laid and get high. Have a cup of tea, too. Tea for two, for one.

Where's the love? Where's the ambition? You see, when I was young… younger… a boy… innocent… none of this seemed obtainable. It was just someone else's bollocks, you understand? No, of course you don't, that's what I mean, what I mean to say, well, here's what I mean… No one understood it, understand? But look what I've done! Power was a rich man's thing back then, when I was a boy; we considered it an achievement if we had power over the TV remote. Politics was just inde… deciph… undeciff… arable… My parents brought me up to think of politicians as stone statues… cold, inhuman and immovable. "They are all chiselled from the same block, Archibald my boy, they are all interchangeable, all you have every election is the chance to rebrand failure." But TV changed that. You people changed that. We slowly killed that notion. Well, not the failure bit – yeah, I will give you that – but the idea that you couldn't be human to do the job. You sculptured me from that same stone and I am every bit as human as you, I am you, I am your creation. We attempted what not so long ago would have been the impossible and we succeeded! Didn't we? Fuck yeah! Why aren't you proud of changing the world? Because the world is shit or because it's ending? Because it's ending, right? Yeah, okay, fair enough. What a shame that is though, don't you think? We are finally living in a country where anything can happen, and the impossible is possible, where a nobody can become a celebrity and a celebrity can become a leader. You can finally extract something out of nothing and everything is ending. That's a shame.

Where is the appreciation and the love for all we've changed? Why doesn't anyone love me any more? You think I'm ineffectual? Well, you wait until the lawyers take over! That's what's going to happen, I've seen them, ssshhh! Keep quiet. They are here. Waiting. Hide your children. Hide your money! They are taking over the country; they're taking over the world! Run! Run while you still can! If they fuck with me, I'm going to use the red phone on their arses... Yeah, I have a red phone. Yeah, a fucking red phone. You've all seen the films, you know about the red phone. You know what I can do with that phone. One word to the right people and it's goodnight, goodnight, thanks for watching and see you after the break.

I did use the red phone once, after a particularly heated argument with some foreign dignitary whose name, and if I'm being honest, country, escapes me. I gave it all the puffed up rhetoric and threats, I stroked the phone receiver, I warned him not to mess with me, but still he carried on, waving his fist and shouting at me, so I picked up the phone. I had no idea who I would speak to or what I would say, but it didn't matter anyway as it was engaged. I found a slightly less gratifying but certainly very effective alternative by slapping him across the face with the receiver.

I suppose it's only predictable that in any vulnerable state you would think about love above all else, and such was the case for me in the back of that car. I thought of my dear Albie. I could think of nothing else and no one more important, for there was no such person. I so dearly needed her embrace at that moment, there in that car; that firm confident hug that made everything else irrelevant and the contact all. I needed to see her, needed one last conversation, to apologise and tell her I love her, but I knew it was impossible. I was a fugitive in my own country, I was a wanted man with a price on my head and wherever she was, it wouldn't be safe for me. Beyond that, of course, was Zach; a six-foot pigeon-chested stumbling block to her even looking me in the eye again. That she had left us both may have been the case but what if Zach was dead? That was a question I have asked myself a lot. If the bastard just disappeared, perhaps we could pick up where we left off, and all would be well? There were so many unanswered questions. The only answer I found myself concluding was that Zach was in the way of my happiness, even if he didn't know it. That being so, I had to see him. I had to talk to him, and if reason does not become reasonable, I would just have to kill him.

As the simple thought of murder occupied my mind, I slept, finding comfort in my curled-up foetal position. I fell back into a dream that used to once be a memory but had passed the point of age where it became a doubt.

I was at my parent's house, back in the over-prepared clothes of the teenager and smelling too much of my father's aftershave, my face smooth still and my hair full of wax that smelled of coconut. My girlfriend Sandy was coming to visit and meet my parents. I had prepped my parents on her first visit and pleaded with them to keep all embarrassing tales and incriminating photos under check and they had promised, but of course they couldn't help themselves when faced with an audience. Not for chatting about the weather my parents. It was sunny when Sandy came for tea that first time; a spring sun full of tantalising promise.

Sandy was chewing over a photo of me having a bath in an old sink when dinner arrived. The photo albums were sat by my mother and she was carefully rifling through them, looking for any of me naked, despite my gentle and polite requests to put them back. Sandy dropped a reassuring hand to my leg from time to time, but the humiliation was complete when the photo of me aged five and three quarters, wearing a polo neck jumper and taking a dump in a watering can, was displayed on the table next to the asparagus. There was great laughter and a tighter squeeze of the leg. I sunk a little lower in my seat and sat in silence for the rest of the meal, allowing the light grilling of Sandy that was inevitable ever since I first mentioned her name to my parents, to start without any interference.

'So what do your parents do, Sandy?' Mother began.

'My dad works in the city. I don't really understand

what he does. It's something about finance,' Sandy said in her watered-down northern lilt.

'Humph,' was my father's response. He had a habit of being able to sum up his feelings on any subject or person with very few words. My mother, on the other hand, liked to try and use as many words as possible which was a way of trying to convince people that she was highly educated and not a dropout at fourteen that worked in a seaside sweet shop before marrying the man who ran the ghost train and achieving the golden career peak of housewife and mother. She would also tell anyone who would listen that she read a lot of books and enjoyed "the classics."

'My mother works with horses.'

'Horses! I love horses! Don't I?' my mother chirped with excitement, looking at my father and I for nods of confirmation. My father grunted at her and then looked at Sandy and offered her the same.

'She runs a small school, she teaches children to ride – adults too, sometimes, but she mainly focuses on children. She works with some children's charities and likes to use horse riding as a kind of therapy. It's amazing how beneficial the children seem to find it. I can't ride myself.'

'I love children! What a wonderful thing to do. Does she make much money doing that?' My mother said, leaning forward and waiting for Sandy's answer. My father had put down his knife and fork and decided to use that moment to take a delicate sip of water in case he missed her answer. My parents, despite claiming for years that they were socialists, had a very unhealthy obsessive jealousy about other people's wealth, and it was forever the one topic that would generate true heated conversation. My father later confessed to me that he only ever claimed to be a socialist because back when he met my mother, all the attractive people were "extreme lefty scruffs that smelt of petunia oil and orange peel" and he figured that women wanted a man who knew their own mind. The truth was that all my mother really wanted back then was a sandwich toaster.

'She does okay, but she doesn't do it for the money. She does it for the children and the fact that she loves horses.' Sandy's reply was polite but uninviting of further questioning. I had mentioned to her what to expect and she seemed to have been revising. My mother leaned back in her chair and studied Sandy's face for a moment before concluding that it was time for dessert and making a hasty exit to the kitchen.

'Still…' sighed my father, through a last mouthful of potato, 'finance. Must do well. Colourful ties.' It was as if a great philosopher had spoken and we ate our dessert in silence.

My parents excused themselves after tea in a rather obvious and loud fashion and decided that the time and weather was right for a leisurely husband and wife walk. Sandy and I looked at each other for a moment wondering whether to take up the baton of opportunity that my parents had clumsily dropped at our feet. We didn't wonder for long. With nervous smiles and sweaty interlocked hands, we stumbled upstairs to do what you did when there was nothing on the TV and you can't find the Ker-Plunk. I was alive with a glorious emotion; that feeling of cradling a velvet heart in thick gloves, that unmistakable hollow hunger, nerve endings alive like exposed electrics, and even now, in my dream states and nightmare realities, I can always recall that feeling. I have spent every year, month and day trying to duplicate it ever since. Even with Albie I couldn't find it. Perhaps it is the sole preserve of the young and the innocent; a feeling a cynical adult frame cannot allow. It is all I envy the young for. Right now, it is all they have in their corner.

When I woke, there was a large fleece coat lying on me and I sat up in it and noticed Edgerton at the boot of the car. He was holding up a small hat with a questioning look. I shook my head and buttoned the coat. We were parked up opposite a small arcade of shops, and to the other side a large park spread out towards a lake. The day had played out its main event and was drawing the curtains to dusk; the shabby gloom rolled over us and cast all obscure. The park and the road were eerily quiet. It was the sort of Sunday morning calm that scared me as a child and terrified me as an adult. I have never quite understood just what it is about Sundays that unnerves me so. I used to assume it was a childhood fear of a soon-returning school day and maybe in part it was that, but as an adult and with the fear now a morbid dread, vile in its predictability, I had no answers for the sheer maudlin feeling that always came, crippling action and adventure and casting me a corpse until it would die out and a new week would be born. For me, the week always started on a Monday and the week ended on a Saturday. Sunday was merely our penance. It was all the more ridiculous an emotion now as it was a Thursday evening.

Edgerton peered into the back seat window and offered a comforting smile, eyeing up the coat and trying, perhaps, to reassure me of my credibility. The coat itched against the skin; I imagined it had fleas. I imagined someone had died in it and the undertakers had to prise the thing off them with a crowbar and an insult to fashion. I considered taking the offer of the hat but thought better of it. I've never been able to work a hat.

'We need some provisions,' Edgerton whispered, his eyes darting up and down the street and past me towards the park. 'You must be hungry.'

'Where are we going?'

'I need to get you safe. It is my calling.'

'Really, you shouldn't feel the need.'

'You talk as if I have some choice in the matter. I have no choice here, Archie.'

'John?'

'John. He told me I had to get the message to the people. It has to be you, Archie.'

'What about Zach? Albie? I think you flatter me in my importance.'

'You are the Prime Minister.'

'Yes, well like I said…'

'We can talk some more on the way. We cannot stay here long. Wait here.'

And with that, with my response half in my mouth and half in my brain, Edgerton wandered off towards a small mini-market on the opposite side of the road, walking with the confidence that only a man who believes in something could possibly have. I slumped back in the back seat like an impertinent child and held the coat around me. The stereo was now playing an advert for a local estate agents' firm and I could feel yesterday's alcohol briefly at the roof of my mouth and the tip of my throat.

I looked back at the park on the other side of road. It seemed to be darker than even evening warranted; somehow the ugly trees positioned around it were hugging out the dusk light, suffocating even the shadows and the small moon lines that sparkled on the lake. For the briefest of moments, it looked like a haunted forest from some children's book, some place of magic and mystery that would contain fire breathing dragons and unicorns, and certainly in my current addled state neither would have been such a stretch. The image was disrupted somewhat by a brilliant pink ice cream van trundling through it at the speed of a stalker, roaming the hill mounds and rounding the trees, on the look out for punter or prey it seemed, but then I told myself I was being ridiculous. That said, for me, ice cream vans sit alongside clowns as a thing of childish joy that carried a vague aroma of the child killer about it. I think I probably had a fairly mixed-up childhood.

A vandalised street sign in front of me showed a painted stick figure hanging from gallows and I imagined it was Zach. Someone had written the word "BYE" twice underneath the figure and I heard myself saying it to Zach as he breathed his last. I looked back across at the mini-market and suddenly felt very alone. That I craved Edgerton's company and that I was sat in a stolen car in a fleece jacket was almost as scary as the realisation of how very far I had fallen so very quickly. Just the previous week, I had had sex with a cultural attaché who dressed up as a nun.

A good ten minutes, which weren't so good, passed and Edgerton still hadn't come out. No one had passed me, I saw no shadow or shape, heard not whisper or scream; there was nothing except the patrolling ice cream van and the occasional small tune coming from a speaker on its roof. I decided to go and find Edgerton, deciding not to think of how contradictory to my feeling about the man that decision was, fastening my coat as tight as I could to preserve my last modicum of dignity and stepping out into the street. At that moment, and with the most extraordinary voluminous bang, like the very gods themselves were blowing up crisp packets and slapping them flat, the mini-market exploded and I flew back over the bonnet of the car, my fleece coat blowing off me and burning away to nothing on the kerb. The car itself shifted sideways and thudded against the wooden barrier to the park, small flames at the tyres and the last glass in the windows now completely gone. An alarm sounded, then two more, shop alarms and car alarms dueting in one utterly tuneless and unnecessary song.

I lay on the street, looking up at a large tree leering over from the park, sheltering me from the stars in the sky, and covering me in its far-reaching gloom. My face was burning hot, my body freezing cold; I shuffled up to a seated position and sat on a shard of glass. The mini-market was aflame, a huge firey gob blurting out through the shopfront, spitting fire and belching smoke. Still no one came. I could see curtains twitching in the flats above the arcade, small slits of light and the odd black shape against each. But nothing stayed; everything went. I stood slowly, dusted my chest down, ran a hand through my hair and across my body, looking for blood or anything loose. I seemed to be intact, together in body, mind and hangover. I picked up the fleece coat and banged it down hard onto the ground to put out the flames, but as I did the coat perished in my hands, each piece wafting to the ground like smoking skin. I looked into the park, at the cool quiet and the gentle space between the trees, and there seemed to be sanctuary in there. I imagined walking into the darkness would seem to be like diving into a pool of water, washing clear the day's blemishes and diseases and renewing you, easing you out into a new world where you could start again with a noble justification. I crossed the wooden barrier and stepped in. Instantly the gloom shrouded me and it felt safe, it felt good; I walked forward and allowed myself to be swallowed whole by the park and the thick pulsing blackness within.

I found a bench and fell on to it face-first and let the tears fall. Whether a painful emotion or an emotion of pain, they were genuine and they were thick and had to play themselves dry. The bench was worn and chipped and a splinter tickled my cheek. The acrid smell of urine wafted upwards from between the gaps in the bench and my nose prickled. But none of this mattered. I was safe. The blackness suddenly seemed appealing. The anonymity, the mystery, the perfect hiding place. With great effort, I rolled onto my side and fell off the bench. My eyes swam in the dark sky. I was at the lowest point of my recent high and my imagination felt stretched and old. I started formulating my last moves. In my mind I sought out my dear friend, and then my precious love, and I knew that survival meant closing one out. There was no logic, yet, and for that reason, no alternative. I closed my eyelids and I slept in the puddle of piss where I lay.

I felt safe in sleep, maybe through the decisions I was making alone in my head or maybe just through the grasp of the certainty of not having many choices open to me any more. When you are Prime Minister, you can do a lot. When you are a wanted man – well, not so much. May as well embrace your two options and give them some thought. As I stirred awake, I found myself in the warm arms of wool almost instantly and stopped still, frozen in the warm sensation and daring not to break it; thick cardigan arms were wrapping themselves around me and hugging me close.

'Albie?' I found myself saying, yet somehow knowing that it simply couldn't be. I breathed in the wool and gripped the arm tight, but despite the comfort it was alien to me. It wasn't Albie.

'See if you can find some clothes in the bag there, Samuel. Have a look.'

I looked up at an early morning sky, diluted to a dishwater smear and etched in a ghostly mist that feathered around me like curious spirits. At my feet sat a little boy burrowing away in a large bag, tossing clothes out like a jumble sale bargain hunter. I then looked up and back at the owner of the woolly arms and found myself staring back at the sweet face of a plain beauty.

She looked slightly regal at first, then as she wrapped me tighter into her rock-face cleavage and wiped away the dribble at my mouth with a multi-purpose, much used tissue, I was put in mind of my old dinner ladies at school, women with easy breasts who smelled of sweet food; how perfect a memory. I was rudely interrupted that indulgence as a pair of trousers were forced onto my legs and yanked upwards with no respect for my position, dignity or bruised testicles, the boy grabbing my legs and forcing a hideous pair of 1970's social worker slacks on me like I was the last mannequin in the shop window.

'Go easy there, Samuel, don't push them all the way up. I'm sure Mr. Butcher can do the rest. You may find the material a tad itchy, Mr. Butcher. It used to bring my father out in a rash. We were just taking this lot to a charity shop. It seems a bit ridiculous perhaps under the circumstances, but what the news has been saying isn't really true, is it? I can't believe it is. At least we have been able to help you. How very fortuitous, wouldn't you say? Just wait until I tell my friends at pilates, they are going to be so jealous. I loved the show, you know? We voted for you fifty times. I'm so happy you were Prime Minister. Just think if that ventriloquist had won! Dear me no, that would have been terrible.'

I leant forward and sneezed blood on her shoes. She didn't seem aware. I suppose cradling a semi-naked celebrity is a lot of people's crowning moment. Stupid bastards.

'Careful there, Samuel, leave the zip alone. Be careful.'

'Yes mummy. Careful as a mouse.'

Are mice careful? I found myself asking my subconscious. Was that ever a trait of theirs so apparent as to be remembered and used as a label? I suddenly had an image of a six-foot mouse leering over me, its pink slab paws lunging for me ready to flatten me and its tombstone teeth ready to bite down and carry me off. Before I could answer my question, the trousers were on and she was trying to strap a belt around me, my feeble protests being batted away by polite laughter and the grating tune of the ice cream van, returning, moving closer and bleating its tinny promise of wondrous delights.

'Can I go and get an ice cream, mummy?'

'Yes, do you have your pocket money?'

'Yes.'

'You're all going to die! It's the end of the world! The end is nigh! Have an ice cream!'

'Don't frighten the boy, Mr. Butcher. He's at a very impressionable age.'

As the boy ran off towards the ice cream van, the woman patted my hair and lifted me up to a seated position, masterfully wedging a large collared off-yellow shirt onto me with ruffles that looked like the shirt's intestines were oozing through, as she did. Everything itched – my arms, my legs, my brain – and I battled against her but I found little left to offer. She seemed to be finding the whole thing very humorous, a dreadfully simpering suburban laugh puffing out of her nose as her fingers played down the buttons of the shirt and caressed me smooth. What a dreary little woman she was, the sort of woman who refuses to put wallpaper in her house lest she disappear completely. Across the grass, the boy was slurping away at an ice cream cone whilst the ice cream man leant out of his hatch like a sideshow act trying to round up the curious, laughing across at me with the sort of raucous laugh that was so scattershot it meant nothing, only that he desired to be noticed. If first impressions meant anything any more, it was possible he was one fruit bowl shy of a banana and, quite frankly, who needs comical input from such a man?

Completing the geography teacher look assembled from the bland bitch's charity bag was a pair of shiny leather shoes with a Cuban heel. I would like to venture I had never looked more ridiculous but we all know that would be a lie. She offered me a cravat and I nearly vomited on her lap.

'You look very swish, Mr. Butcher.'

'Swish? Who ever uses the word "swish" anymore? You are really saying I look fucking stupid, aren't you?'

'I really don't care for the language...'

'I look like a sitcom pimp.'

'I don't know what that means. My father wore those when he was courting my mother.'

'It's a wonder you were ever born, darling.'

'Excuse me?'

'You have a car?'

'A car, yes, I have a car.'

'Give me the keys.'

'Why?'

'Because I'm your Prime Minister! I'm your Prime Minister and I command you to give me your car keys!'

'I will not! Now, Samuel and I have some errands to run, we would happily give you a lift after that if you…'

I grabbed her bag and yanked it off her shoulder, upending the contents on to the bench. She started hitting me and screaming but I was consumed and nothing could drag me back. The keys landed on the ground and as I bent to pick them up she stamped on my hand. The boy was shouting now too; just behind his voice was the gibbering caterwauling that surely belonged to the ice cream man. Still I ploughed on, ignoring all, most of all myself. I grabbed the keys in a fist, brushed her too-conventional shoe weapon to one side, and then swung the fist out to the three of them that were now gathered around me like a hungry mob. The woman activated her rape alarm but no one came. The ice cream man made to lunge for me but I brought the fist in to his side and he fell. The boy was ducking down behind the bench, crying and hiding, his ice cream now a creamy wound on his shirt.

I started to back away from them, tottering in the Cuban heels and swinging my arm in front of me like I was trying to guide them all back down to earth. I felt exhilarated, alive and primed. It was the closest I have ever got back to the feeling I had walking up those stairs with Sandy all those years ago. Suddenly the mists, self-inflicted or suffered, the open wound of my life and the black rip of my yearning, all seemed to wither away and Zach and Albie became all. I recalled the hollowness of those nights where I had to endure Albie returning home to him, those dreadful waking hours of paranoia and loathing that sent me into every personal spiral possible. The hours I spent half awake in a state of fake detachment, falling in and out of bottles and snorting up everything illegal I could find. I cried more on those nights than I ever had before. That horrible situation, that vile and evil situation that could never produce good, but I had no choice but to live in. That's my love story. That was the only justification I could offer the three of them. It was also the only fuel I needed to see my task through.

I found her car and fell in, locking the doors and ignoring her thumps on the window. I punched the car out of the car park, clipping the gate and snapping off the wing mirror and then I was out, mounting the curb and swinging the car out across lanes until I was set on course for Apple Avenue. I passed the mini-market and my mind leaned back to the scene in my hotel room yesterday, and dear old Edgerton now scattered to the four winds and no doubt being hoovered up into a bag, waving around the envelope at me, the blood on his arms and hands disappearing as quickly as it came. His talk of wonders within and the sheer joy on his face – had the lunatic been right? Had something glorious happened that we all missed? Edgerton was a two-bit palm-reading shyster from a seaside resort now closed for half the year, why would such great truths be bestowed on him? I was the Prime Minister and people wanted to kill me. Hardly fair, was it? The mini-market was now a blackened charred mess and I could see well-dressed men outside as if on guard. The suits were of the most exorbitant style and wealth, the hair held in place by sheer will and fear. The shoes shone even from this distance. Men were wandering in and out of the building; some spoke together in small huddles, others pointed up and down the road. They seemed to be anxious and searching, annoyed and frustrated. Passing the mini-market and surveying the carnage, I felt enormous freedom cover me. I felt released and renewed and, more than anything, responsibility was now off my shoulders and that was the greatest freedom of all. I could do anything, I could go anywhere and I could be anyone and, if Punkley had been right, I could get away with it too. It made perfect sense. Still does, if you're asking.

I paid no attention to the lights as I drove and even less to other driver's and they responded in kind; somehow common courtesy seemed facetious in our helter-skelter free for all dance, and I got to Apple Avenue in under ten minutes, pulling up just as the road bends in and the houses begin. I looked up to Zach's house and saw no car in the drive, no windows open, no life within, and looking further along I could see people standing in their doorways, staring blankly up to the sky, neighbours and friends not talking despite their common interests and fears. One couple were rowing over a fence but that was as close as closeness got. I looked back to the start of the avenue and saw the old alleyway running along behind the back gardens, an alleyway I had walked along so many times before, and now knew I would again, one last time. I began to wish I had taken the hat from Edgerton just for the extra bit of anonymity. I hadn't considered what might happen were I seen. Well, that's not strictly true, I knew the answer; just not how I would deal with the question.

I walked down the alley and stopped behind the shed in the back of Zach and Albie's garden. I'd stopped there before, many times, checking house for sound or movement and found myself doing the same now, even though I didn't care whether there was either. I took a moment, leaning against the shed, to stockpile every negative thought I could find that would get me in the door. In the end it was horribly easy, too easy for a friendship that had promised so much. But my thoughts of Albie covered all and it was very simple, suffocating out Zach's face. I stood and walked in to the back garden. The back door was open, yawning against the hinges and the early morning rain-freckled breeze. I entered the kitchen and, without even thinking, reached into the knife drawer and pulled out the biggest and sharpest knife I could find. I stood still for a second, feeling the weight of the knife and listening for sounds, suddenly feeling a little unsure and embarrassed – an emotion I knew well, but I had no idea why it felt it had the right, right then.

Their house was not much to look at, particularly when you consider the money they had earned over the years and the jobs they had done. Albie liked it that way; she liked the normality, the sense of not getting too far above your station. She had been the one to instigate the move from the country once we entered government; she said it was important not to live grand and that we should be in touch with the voters. Stupid woman. Zach would have continued playing the "manor in the country" card but in the end he would fit into her life however she wanted. She had that power and she hated it. I crossed the kitchen into the lounge; everything was frighteningly tidy and organised. Papers were symmetrical on the living room table, books neatly stacked according to size on the shelves, furniture carefully placed in the appropriate groove in the carpet. There was no sign of Zach. There was no sign of anyone. As I looked deeper into the house, I realised that there was no sign of Albie either. Literally and figuratively. The books were Zach's, the ornaments too; there were great missing pieces of a life there. Every trace of a woman's touch seemed to have deserted the house. She may only have just left him, but if anything could be read from standing in a person's house, you would swear that she had never even been there in the first place.

I wandered upstairs, straining to hear anything except the low rhythm of my heartbeats, the knife in a sweaty grip and resting against a leg. I entered the bathroom and that too was spotless and barren; a small family of rubber ducks lined the side of the bath in order of seniority and height. Male cosmetics were positioned on a shelf in a small circular pattern. I caught sight of myself in the bathroom mirror and looked away in disgust, knowing that any deliberation, any reveal, would finish me. I ploughed on through the spare bedrooms, kicking each door open, expecting to see him and have him launch himself at me and I held the knife ready each time, jabbing it into empty air and staring back into ordered, clinical rooms.

I walked back along the landing and stopped at the master bedroom – a room I knew quite well. A room where I had risen high and fallen hard. The door was ajar and I gently pushed it open with a foot, the knife held in front of me at chest height, ready for the kill, the childish excitement of possibility welling inside me. The bed was made and the pillows positioned neatly against the headboard. At the end of the bed, a TV was sat on a stand, a series of wires running out of the back and disappearing into the wall. I could see the flashes of the picture playing against the dull magnolia wall opposite but heard no sound. Rounding the TV and sitting on the edge of the bed, I saw myself looking back at me from the TV, not though, addressing the country but rather undressing Albie. We were in this very room, passionately kissing, adult caresses, impatient and greedy humans, hungry and lost. We fell onto the bed, rolling into the duvet and ripping at each other's clothes and then, as the memory kicked in, I had to look away, reaching a hand to the TV screen to stop myself buckling to the ground, disgust and desire proving themselves more uneasy bedfellows by far. I tried to turn the TV off but found no switch, then found no point. I coughed up blood onto the carpet and tears sprang to my eyes, my fingers burying deep inside to stop them but missing every time. Somehow the truth of what I was watching made me want to scream and stick the knife into myself there and then. If I were to go out, then why not here? Suddenly, as carefully as I had built my stupid reasoning up, and had formulated my scattershot plans for murder and love, they all fell about me like a castle built from matchsticks, quickly engulfed by one careless hand. I couldn't think and I couldn't breathe and I knew that I had to do at least one.

I ran downstairs, stumbling at the bottom and

falling flat on the carpet. A phone was ringing somewhere, the sound making me jump in and out of my skin, and then, just as I was at the door and turning the handle, I heard her. It was Albie, the small tinny mechanical voice not hiding that beautiful accent, yet she was far away and she was talking to Zach. She was talking love and offering contrition. I gagged and opened the door into my face. The knife bedded into the frame and as I yanked it free, wood splintered with it. I swayed out into the driveway, fumbling the car keys as I walked across people's gardens back to the car. The knife landed in the footwell and tears on my vulgar clothes. Fury was blasting through me like a fractured oil well, filling up my head and hijacking every thought. I started the car and reversed out, swinging it forward as I hit the main road, punching the accelerator to the floor. I had no idea where to go, so I ended up going backwards.

Mr. Laker's car was out front and everything seemed to be in place. The old sign "Laker & Butcher Plumbing Services" still sat at the crooked angle above the first portakabin and, although the industrial estate seemed deserted, a few lights shone forth, promising life somewhere or other. I must have been parked up outside for an hour or two, just staring at my old haunt like a ghost trying to fit back in. I couldn't think where else to go. I could think of no one else that would welcome me.

More worryingly, though, I could think of nothing to say to the old man, so I just sat there some more, letting my mind empty and hoping for inspiration to fill it up.

Looking back, I don't know what I could rationally have expected from him, whether any more than a customary welcome, I couldn't say, but to be greeted by my former boss and mentor with a punch to the face was certainly the last. I lay there amongst a carpet of invoices and folders, my nose bleeding across my face, a tooth dislodged and spat on to the floor and old man Laker pulled up a chair and sat over me, his crazy pensioner hair up at every angle like his very words were giving him electrical shocks.

'What the bloody hell do you think you're doing, Archie?'

'I… I wanted… Can I still have my old job back?'

'Have it back? You never resigned in the first place! Oh, it's all right for you young 'uns running off with your fanciful ideas and desires. Some of us have a responsibility. If you wanted to be Prime Minister, Archie, why didn't you just ask? But no, not you. Imagine Hilda's and my surprise when we turn the TV on and see you doing some second-rate Sinatra…'

'It was Bing Crosby –'

'Shut up. And let it be said that was one shit programme, Archie. It was fixed, wasn't it? That spoon player was a fucking genius – far better than you.'

'I'm sorry Mr. Laker.'

'Oh, you are? Well that's the first step on a long road, is it not?'

'I just want to go back to how things were. You and me.'

'There is no you and me. I've retired.'

'Can I –'

'I'm not responsible for you any more. You do what you want. I hear you're good at that.'

'I just want to be normal.'

'Needs work, kid. Needs a lot of work.'

The opposite lane of traffic was thick with cars, loaded up with luggage and fearful faces, as I drove. People seemed desperate to be elsewhere, yet I could think of only one place to be. Even though I was travelling the well-worn journey back to my old home, it was only when I was entering the village that I actually realised where I was. People were pouring out of houses in a congested impatience, bags and belongings weighing down their escape. The village green was thick with huddled groups whispering conspiratorial nothingness and waving their arms to an unseen anyone in front of them. Two minibuses were being loaded up with people and things, and I watched as they all crammed in there like it were a portable coffin, wondering in amazement at some of the things they were taking with them. You can tell a lot about a person by the things they deem worthy of saving; indeed at such a time as this you are really able to see people for what they truly are. I saw nothing.

I trundled past my old house, the brilliant soothing blue that my wife had mocked so often still shining out like a beacon welcoming me home, and I mounted the pavement outside and cut the engine. The front door was open and a family were leaving the house, laden down with bags. A mother was dragging a screaming child and the child, in turn, was dragging a compliant rag doll. They bundled themselves into a waiting car where a man watching his watch seemed to be fretting about time. The car screeched away and the last I saw was the child's face contorted with tears as she looked back at my house, her home no more. The house looked complacent, but the front garden was a mess. Upstairs, a window clearly needed fixing. It was harmed, but I understood it and that was enough.

Across the road, amongst the huddled masses dictating their lives into the widest circle, I could see a small figure, a woman, sat scrunched up at one end of the bandstand, her legs pulled to her chest and her head buried in either book or prayer. The old bastard from number 52 was standing in front of her, seemingly trying to beckon her away, to make something known that she clearly had no interest in knowing. I rolled the window down to try and hear better what they were saying, but I heard only one thing: 'Fuck off, you oyster-bollocked twat,' and then the conversation was over and the old man was scuttling away. A smile broke on my face and I let it hang there a minute, enjoying the responsibility. She was in the shade of the bandstand roof, her body an outline, her hair possessing shine enough to break through and imprint on the eyes. I found myself lost in her, willing her to notice me, wondering if she would care if she did, or would I just be another pair of male eyes to divert away? I found myself wanting to know her name; I wanted to call to her, shout hello, but the fear of who I was, what I had become and all that I didn't know, stopped me. Instead, I turned back to the house, got out of the car, retrieved the knife from the footwell and entered the front door.

So much had changed. The furniture and décor were different but there was still a feel that remained, a warming embrace of smells and images that had forever infested themselves into the walls. I had been so happy here. I walked the rooms, poking in stranger's cupboards and drawers, lying on their bed and smelling their stale odours in the duvet, the smell of desperately conventional sex that is born the moment you stop moving. I stood at the bedroom window and looked back down at the bandstand and at the woman's outline. From here, her back was to me and I could see she was reading, never moving or shifting, lost in fiction, her temporary reality.

I kicked off the heels and slumped back onto the bed, allowing myself to sleep into the night and dream into dawn. When I awoke the sun was beaming in, dust particles dancing in the promising shards, and the room was thrown alive in the ushering arm of a clear and crisp day. I stretched and let things click back into place, then swung myself out of bed and raided what food they had left for breakfast, hungrily cramming down whatever was to hand. I had a shower and checked their cupboards for any clothes that might fit me and didn't require bravery to wear, but I found very little. As the morning fell over itself, I went back to the bedroom window and looked to the bandstand. She was back in place, huge sunglasses on her face hiding her from the world. That morning, the green was almost free of people; only a few wandered about aimlessly, unsure of where to go, staring up at the sky and at people they once knew. The next morning it was the same, only the few had dwindled to a couple, an old couple, and to me and the girl at the bandstand. The next day I saw only her, thought only of her and needed no more. It was frighteningly easy, back at that house, to shut out even the most recent of histories. I was in a corruptible memory and players were by invitation. Yes, it was fake, but I had had my fill of reality. That was for others.

I spent the morning wandering about the house, sorting the leftover furniture into my own design; I fixed a shelf and pulled up some weeds in the garden. I spent the afternoon in the attic rifling through what they had left; old photos, some books, old furniture, children's toys and then, sat at the back on its own, looking like the last kid to get picked for the sports team, I saw my old award, the imitation gold paint now flecked and peppering the metal wrench, dulled perceptibly, but still trying to look important, sat there on the cheap plastic base, my name underneath hiding under a smear of neglect. I took it out of the attic and put it up on a shelf above the bed, diligently buffing it to a shine and gazing back at it proudly, ashamed that I had forgotten it all those years ago yet happy that I wasn't deemed important enough for someone to sell it.

I watched her read the books closed, coming from an unseen place to the bandstand at the same time every morning, trudging across the green in battered trainers, her books in hand and her sunglasses on her face hiding every emotion like she were behind a screen. I saw no one else for over a week; it was just me and her in a crafted world where no one else belonged. The rest of this place had run away, the bloodhounds screaming the end, yet she still had books to read. I determined to meet her, prepared to suffer the kill that would surely come. I straightened my stupid clothes, ran a comb through my hair and stared back at myself in the bathroom mirror just long enough for my eyes to betray and then I was out of the front door, approaching the bandstand.

I stopped about ten feet away. Her back was to me, her face in the book, the sound of the day emptied into the pocket of the night. There were no birds in the sky, nothing on the horizon, nothing behind or about; my ghost town closing down just in a perfect moment.

'You will hate me, everyone does,' she said, and I smiled.

'Maybe you will hate me too. You would be in good company.'

'Sure wouldn't want that. It's the last original idea we have left, you know? The idea of the individual.'

'Would you like a cup of tea?'

'I would, yeah. But...'

'But?'

'Everything is shit. Isn't it?'

'I'm afraid it is.'

'But maybe tomorrow?'

'What happens tomorrow?'

'Who knows? But today is perfect. If there isn't a tomorrow, at least we will always have the perfection of not hating each other today.'

'I've not had that before.'

'I'm not sure I have either.'

'Until tomorrow, then?'

She nodded her head without turning round. It may have been the result of a laugh – I like to think not, I refuse to believe it was – and then she stood and left the bandstand without looking back. I turned back to the house, never once looking around, frightened that there would be something to see.

That night I was restless and fevered; I woke frequently and eventually conceded to it and went downstairs for a glass of water. Sitting in a cold moonlight wash at the kitchen table, I listened to the sound of gunfire in the distance, trying to work out how far away it was and if it was getting nearer or further away. I turned a radio on when it all got too much, to drown out the noise, and got nothing but interference. Eventually I just covered my ears, hoping that it would all go away. I fell asleep at the table that way, just for a moment, swaying in my seat and dribbling down my chin. It was the sound of a car pulling up and braking harshly just outside that snapped me awake like a slap in the face and I jumped up, knocking over the chair, and stumbled back out of the moonlight, into the shadows, peering behind the kitchen curtains out at the night, and trying to stabilise my funky heart. A solitary figure was standing by the postbox on the corner of the street, his face turned upwards to the top floor of my house. He was just a shape, just a shadow thrown by my mind, perhaps, but it was Zach, of that I was sure; I felt for the knife but it was not there; I weaved a hand into the nearest drawer but all I found was a spoon. My defeat was surely nearly complete. I watched him watching my house for maybe a minute or two and then he moved away, back to the car, got in and drove away and silence fell like a soft blanket.

It was the first time I had thought of Zach since

being back at the house, the first time I had considered what I had become whilst breathing in what I used to be, and I resented him for bringing reality back to me. With reality came Albie and I was forced to create hatred again like it was my masterful design. I can't outrun anything any more, I know that, and hatred is handy for survival. It is easier for me to beat out love from the empty void of my heart than it is to find room for it to grow; better to chisel perfection from it than allow my fumbling bloody hands to break it into a lie.

I entered this morning's daylight as confused by life as much as when I first remembered it, but that's okay because I understand confusion so I wasn't going to let it destroy me. There was no point any more. I showered vigorously and then cleaned the kitchen, separated out the teabags left that were still in date and then waited for time to blunder on. I keep the kitchen knife attached to the belt of these ghastly-looking trousers now. I keep seeing Zach's face in the shadows and I keep hearing things too. As I showered, I was convinced that someone was in my bedroom, so I locked the door, wrapped a towel around me and hid in the bathroom for over an hour, listening through the wall to these strange noises coming from the other side, trying to separate them from the ominous sounds breaking over the horizon and find the courage to go on. I found myself praying that something would happen, that something on the other side would make me do something and move me forward. Finally, when I found the courage, I unlocked the bathroom door, stood slowly, and then with all I had left I jumped out onto the landing, my towel falling around my ankles as I did, and kicked the bedroom door open. The room was empty and I was alone. There was nothing on the other side.